MW00952797

Johnny's Reptile Adventure

By C.S. CROOK

Copyright © 2013 by Carolyn Sue Crook

The right of Carolyn Sue Crook to be identified as the Author of Work has been asserted by her in accordance with the Copyright, Designs and Patents Act 1988.

All rights reserved, no part of this publication may be reproduced, stored in a retrieval system, or transmitted in any form or by any means, electronic, mechanical, photocopying, recording, or otherwise, without prior written permission of the Author. This book may not be lent, resold, hired out or otherwise disposed of by way of trade in any form of binding or cover other than in which it is published, without the prior written consent of the Author.

This book is a work of fiction. Names, characters, businesses, places, events and incidents are either the products of the author's imagination or are used in a fictitious manner. Any resemblance to actual persons, living or dead, events or locales is entirely coincidental.

Carolyn Sue Crook. Johnny's Reptile Adventure

This is a heartwarming nature series about a little boy who longs for a dog of his own and an elderly man who is forced to give up his beloved pet. Johnny moves from the desert of West Texas to the West Coast fishing village, Fort Bragg, California, and has to leave behind dear friends and his only pet a horned toad. Just up the road from Johnny's new home, he discovers a scary looking dilapidated old house. There he finds an elderly, grumpy man who has a dog named Trouble. The man tries to scare Johnny away, but Johnny does not scare easily. Later, in 'The Heroic Dog and Boy', Johnny goes back to visit the elderly man and realizes that something is very wrong. The man's dog is straining against its chain and barking wildly at the house. Later, in 'The Magic Wishbone', Hazel, one of Johnny's new friends, makes a wish for the first time ever on Thanksgiving Day, with her mother using a magic wishbone. She refuses to say what she wished for and insists that the magic needs time to happen, although she doesn't understand exactly how magic works. In 'Johnny's Treasure Adventure', Johnny and his friends help to solve a mystery which spans beyond a century, when they find buried treasure near the beach. Together, with the help of the police department, they find answers for how the treasure wound up where it did and who it belonged to. But there is one piece of jewelry in the treasure chest that turns out to have a ghost attached to it. The ghost makes it frighteningly clear that no one else is to have the ruby necklace. This series is about friendships and difficult decisions. It is also about family and how hard it is to move away from dear friends. Step into Johnny's world and follow him on his adventures where the wildlife and scenery comes vividly alive. This series is packed with action and drama, but most of all, it about people caring about and for one another. In this series you will find horned toads, rattlesnakes, raccoons, birds, ponies, fish and a slug, which are all a good mix for children with inquisitive minds.

There are six books in 'Johnny's Adventure' series; #1 'Johnny's Reptile Adventure', #2 'The Skipper's Captain', #3 'The Heroic Dog and Boy', #4 'Finding A Home', #5 'The Magic Wishbone', and #6 'Johnny's Treasure Adventure'.

For Bill, the love of my life.

For Sean and Vanessa, our amazing children.

For all of whom have always encouraged and believed in me.

Contents

Chapter 1

This was going to be yet another brand new adventure for Johnny. He had never lived in the desert before. He had been sitting next to his mother Lilly for hours on the bus when it finally rolled to a stop at their destination. They stepped off the bus with their sparse belongings and stood beside an old mailbox. Before them was a long dirt lane with rows of cotton on either side for as far as the eye could see. His mother smiled brightly at Johnny and said, "It sure feels good to be off that bus."

"You can say that again, Mom. Where are we going? I don't see anything out here." Johnny looked around himself apprehensively.

"I'm sure we will find a house at the end of this lane. There is a mailbox here. Come on let's go and find out." She smiled encouragingly and together they set off down the country lane.

Two little boys stepped from out of the rows of cotton and ran up the lane to meet them. Breathlessly, the older of the two asked, "Are you folks going to be some of our new pickers?"

Lilly responded, "I hope to be. That is why we are here."

The older boy said, "I'm James and this is my brother Robert."

Lilly said, "I'm Lilly and this is my son Johnny."

James said, "We are sure happy to see another kid out here. Come on, I'll take you to see Grandpa. He is the foreman out here."

"Your grandpa is the boss man?" Johnny asked.

"He isn't really my grandpa that is just what everyone calls him," James replied.

As the small group approached a set of irrigation pumps, Johnny could see an older, stocky gentleman bent over working on the pumps with a variety of tools strewn about upon the ground.

Robert sprinted ahead of the group and said, "Grandpa, we found new pickers for you."

Grandpa looked up from his work and saw the woman and her child for the first time. He straightened his back and tossed a wrench to the ground. "Is that so, Robert?" Robert shook his head in affirmation. Grandpa smiled warmly at Lilly and said, "Are you afraid of hard work?"

"No sir, I'm not. I've worked hard my whole life. I've never had anything handed to me, sir. I would be very much obliged if you would be so kind as to give me an opportunity to prove that to you."

She spoke with determination and Grandpa liked that about her. "I will give you that opportunity then," he said, and Grandpa saw her face instantly become radiant. "We have a little shack that you and your boy can stay in over yonder. You folks can take your meals with me and Buster's family. We share grub and cooking together. The other hands stay in a bunk on the other side of the field. They are on their own. Follow me and I will show you to your new home. It is not much but you'll get used to it after awhile."

"I can't tell you how grateful I am, sir."

"You can just call me Grandpa. You don't need to call me sir. Well there it is. It is that third one on the end."

"That is a welcome sight." Lilly said.

"Did you travel far?"

"We traveled far enough to be tired of that bus."

Grandpa left them to rest and to get settled in. That evening Grandpa introduced Johnny and Lilly to Buster and Beth, who were the parents of the two boys. Lilly and Beth took an instant liking to each other. And Johnny soon became like a younger brother to

James and Robert. The three of them spent long hours playing together.

James and Robert had dogs and Johnny really liked dogs. He often dreamed that someday he would have his very own, but for now Robert and James were happy to share theirs with him. He would play fetch with the dogs, throwing a stick for them until his arm was sore from it.

James was always thinking up new games and things for them to do. But one of James favorite things was to play tricks on both Robert and Johnny. But on this one particular day it was Johnny's turn to take the brunt of James's sense of fun. Johnny's legs were long for a five and a half year old, but they just couldn't gobble up the distance across the desert sand as quickly as Robert's seven year old and James's nine year old legs.

James hollered back over his shoulder, "We're going to leave you behind, and the goats and snakes are going to get you."

Robert looked over at James apprehensively. James gave him a wink. James was quite pleased with his new ability to wink. He had to go to great lengths to explain to Robert that when he winked it meant that they were playing a trick on Johnny, which was their favorite pastime. Robert was visibly relieved when he saw James wink.

Johnny made his little legs go even faster. He didn't know which he feared the most, the goats or the snakes. As far as he was concerned they were both deadly. He had no past experience with snakes but had a few close calls with that mean old billy goat, Rex, at the camp. His horns were huge and his eyes, those yellow eyes, were scary. Grandpa had put a bell on him so you could hear him when he tried to sneak up on you.

Johnny kept his eyes glued to the ground as he ran; only glancing up once in a while to check on the position of the older boys. "You guys, wait up." He was getting tired but he wasn't about to give up. They weren't going to leave him out here alone. Not if he could help it.

Up ahead he could see the fields, but they were still far away. There could be a lot of snakes between where he was and where his mama was. He wished she was right there with him. Suddenly, it happened, he fell face first into the sand. There was a cloud of dust that puffed up to greet him. He hadn't been crying. He's found from past experience that it slowed him down. He lifted his face off the desert floor and saw his playmates in the distance. They were nearly to the fields. So now, no matter how hard he tried, he could not hold back the tears. They coursed down his dusty cheeks in crystal rivulets, pattering dark little circles upon the sand as they dripped from his chin.

The harder he tried to stifle the tears, the faster they flowed, flooding down his cheeks. Tears of terror, for he was sure Rex would find him any moment now. This terrifying thought motivated him and he sprung up off his belly as quickly as a deer leaping a fence and continued running.

Blindly, he ran in the direction of his mother, heedless of the snakes. He called to her between his sobs. All he wanted was her. She was all he wanted in the whole wide world.

Lilly heard the ruckus and looked up from the cotton plant that she was plucking the soft little tufts of cotton from. Beth's two boys came running up to the edge of the field next to the irrigation pumps and let their long legs crumble underneath them. They fell to the ground, gasping for breath and laughing wildly, clapping each other on the backs. Lilly saw her Johnny off in the distance running toward her, running and stumbling to the ground and then getting back up to run some more. Lilly looked over at Beth, who was watching her own two boys. Beth's lips were pressed into a straight thin line. Her eyes narrowed, and her hands were fists pressed into her hips. Lilly knew holy heck was about to break loose. James was the first to look over at Beth. He could see the veins at her temples pulsate, the way they always did when she was just about to blow. His eyes bulged out the instant this visual image registered in his brain. His face fell quiet, instantly. Her gaze fixed with his and he froze.

4

"I want you two young ones to know that the minute Grandpa gets back, you're both going to get a licking. He's never here anymore when you need him."

Her glare turned to Robert and instantly softened. He was young and very often misled by his fun-loving, bigger brother. Unfortunately, the fun always seemed to be at Johnny's expense.

"Beth, you can't go so hard on the boys." Lilly walked up and laid a soft hand upon Beth's shoulder.

Beth turned and quickly searched Lilly's face. Lilly knew how much she hated to spank the boys; how much she hated the guilt that followed. They had talked like many good friends do about such things. But Beth was also resolved to stop James's behavior, to break the pattern. She prayed she could.

"You're both grounded all day tomorrow."

"Oh, Momma, that's unfair!" Robert cried.

"You're going to be grounded all day today and the day after tomorrow too, if I hear any more whimpering."

"Don't do that, I'll be good," Robert wailed.

Lilly could feel a smile spread across her lips. It was a good feeling. It tugged gently at the corners of her mouth. She straightened her face, but Beth saw it and a smile burst across her face, too. Beth nodded in Johnny's direction and together the two of them set out to meet him.

"I'm going to straighten those two out, yet."

"Amen," Lilly sighed, wistfully. Johnny was about ten yards from her now.

"The snakes and goats are going to get me, Momma!" Johnny sobbed, running with outstretched arms toward his mother. His tears, like perfect teardrops, ran together, melding into a stream that ran off his freckled chin. He impacted with her then and his thin little arms wrapped around her legs as he clung to her for dear life.

5

Lilly reached down and softly pried him from her legs and picked him up. She knew that too soon from now she would no longer be able to do this.

Johnny nestled his face into her shoulder and cried in long and hard, heartbroken wails. His friends had let him down. He knew they were his friends, but they had let him down anyway, which made him cry even harder.

Beth reached out and rubbed his back with her fingertips, just the way he liked it. Johnny loved Beth and he knew she loved him too.

He snuggled into his mother's arms. Here he was safe, and he began to settle down and yawned.

"I'll fix him some shade," Beth said, squeezing his shoulder gently. She set up a crumbling piece of sheetrock against a couple of old poles and laid down a couple of clean gunnysacks on the little cot that they kept out in the field for the kids to nap on. She motioned for Lilly to bring him on over.

Lilly smiled appreciatively and walked with him as lightly as a cat. He had just started to nod off. He had had such a hard day. She knew how much he loved Beth's two boys, how lonely he had always been as an only child and how much his friends meant to him. His peaceful, sleeping face was that of pure, sweet innocence. She laid him down on Beth's makeshift bed. He stirred briefly, but settled down when Lilly brushed his brow with her lips. "Shush," she whispered, and his face calmed.

"Well, look who we have here, Lilly." Beth motioned with her right arm toward the left of the field, making a mock bow. Lilly looked up and saw Grandpa walking toward them. He was carrying a bucket.

"Now don't you two girls go poking fun at me? I got myself some lemonade made out of real Texas lemons in this here bucket."

"Grandpa's got lemonade," James shouted, and he scrambled up in a hurry from where he was sitting. Robert followed in hot pursuit. "Grandpa, that's my favorite," Robert panted, when he reached Grandpa's side. Grinning, Grandpa roughed up Robert's hair.

6

"Where did you happen upon some real Texas lemons?" Beth said with her eyes shining brightly, with just a hint of mischief.

"Oh, I got my connections."

"Can we have some, Grandpa?" Robert pleaded, tugging on Grandpa's sleeve.

"Why, I reckon you can child, go get your cups."

Beth peered into the bucket and saw bits of ice floating among the slices of lemon. "I see ice in that bucket. Now I know of only one icebox within fifteen miles of this here cotton patch." Her eyes still twinkled.

Grandpa said, "Would you please go fetch the ladle, Beth?" Beth smiled and walked over to where they kept the lunch boxes and removed the ladle from the water bucket.

"Beth, could you get our cups, please?" Lilly asked.

"Sure, Lilly."

"Ah, shade." Grandpa sighed as he sank down on the ground at the end of Johnny's cot.

Beth smiled and shook her head hopelessly. "That's all you're good for anymore you old goat, finding shade."

"I'm older and wiser now, child. Give it a good stir; the sugar has settled to the bottom of that bucket."

The two boys were already waiting by the lemonade. Beth stirred it until the little whirlpool around the handle of her ladle widened and lapped at the walls of the bucket. She whacked the ladle smartly a couple of times on the rim of the bucket. "There, I reckon that should do it." The two boys crowded their cups toward her, one cup bumping the other. "There's plenty for everyone. Don't be shoving each other."

"James is the one shoving, Mama," Robert hollered. Robert's deep chocolate eyes left the bucket for only an instant to flicker across

James's face to read the expression there. James's eyes were fixed intently on the bucket and his tongue slowly snaked out and swept across his upper lip. There was nothing Robert could say that was going to break that concentration.

Beth let a ladle full of lemonade fall into James cup and then the next into Robert's. James guzzled his down before Beth had Robert's filled and eagerly held his cup out to her for more, while he ran the back of his free hand across his mouth. Beth paused before filling his cup again and looked at him quizzically.

"I'm thirsty, Ma!"

"I can see that," Beth smiled at him tenderly. She scooped up more of the bitter sweet beverage and filled his cup to the brim. She watched as he turned the cup up to his lips and guzzled again in hasty thirst. The excess dribbled from the corners of his mouth. Beth loved these special moments out here on the desert, the almost magical moments that only Grandpa seemed to be able to provide. It wasn't the treats as much as it was the feeling of belonging, belonging together; all of them.

Lilly took Grandpa's cup from Beth and took it over to the old man and sank down into the shade next to him. "I must be getting older and wiser too."

Grandpa looked over at her and smiled, "Just wiser."

"Oh, I don't know, Grandpa. Since I've come here I feel like I've gotten a hundred times older, sometimes."

"Remember just one thing; you're only as old as you are in your mind. Never take it for granted. I'm still twenty-something," he said with a twinkle in his eyes.

Lilly's dimples sparked the tips of her smile, and she reached over and patted Grandpa on the leg nearest to her. She was fond of this old man. "Tell me about the ocean, Grandpa; tell me just one more time."

Grandpa reached over and returned her pat. "The coolness of it; always so cool, it was. That's what I remember the most. I remember the cool breezes and the great blue expanse of the sea, and the sun seems to just slip off, right off the edge of earth. A sunset over the ocean is like nothing you've ever seen, Lilly. The sky is on fire with reds and oranges, and all around that is pink and gold."

"What's the name of that little town again, Grandpa?"

"Fort Bragg, and there are trees there that look just like something out of that story about that giant and the bean stalk. Those trees just seem to go right up into the clouds. It's so cool there that you hardly ever need to sweat, even when you're hauling in those giant redwood logs. That was the most dangerous work I ever did, falling those trees. I loved it there," Grandpa said as he gazed out over the cotton patch to the desert beyond.

Lilly studied the profile of his face for a few moments in the peaceful silence that fell between the two of them. There was a sad look on his old and weather-beaten face. Lilly reached out and touched him softly on his arm and said, "Grandpa, why did you leave there? You loved it so much."

He turned his head to face her again and he smiled a tired, old smile, but the sadness didn't leave his eyes. "Those were the best of times, Lilly, and the worst of times. Sometimes, honey child, you just got to get up and go."

She turned her cup up and downed the rest of what was left in the bottom of it. "That sure was the best lemonade I've ever had," she said standing up.

Grandpa smacked his lips and held his cup out to her. "Can you fetch me another cup?" Lilly nodded and took his cup and walked over to the bucket.

"I'd be careful how much of that I'd let him have, if I were you, Lilly," Beth said as she sat down next to Grandpa in the shade where Lilly had been.

"Why's that Beth?" Lilly looked over at the two of them.

"Why? He's sour enough! That's why."

"There you go picking on a poor old man, again. Buster ought to make you toe the line. You're too dang spirited, Beth." Grandpa looked at her, trying to look mean. The two women laughed and Lilly handed him his cup. Grandpa nodded his thanks as he took it. "Now, this here woman knows how to treat a man, Beth. You should take notice of this. She's always sweet to me. Not ornery like you."

"Can I have some more, Mama?" James asked.

"Yes, but this is the last for you. We need to save some for Johnny. And this here is thirds for you." Lilly filled James cup for the last time and then once again for Robert.

They heard the dogs start to bark and all of them looked in the direction of the camp. "I wonder what's gotten into them," Lilly asked of no one in particular.

Beth shook her head. "I don't know, but they sure are making a racket."

Grandpa stood up, "There's something going on; hear their bark? It's different, I reckon we had better go and find out."

Chapter 2

Beth saw Lilly look apprehensively at Johnny, who was still sound asleep. Beth stood up and pressed the palms of her hands into the small of her back, arching her spine forward and said, "I think he'll be fine, we're going to be right back, Lilly." Lilly nodded and they all set out together; the two boys ran ahead.

Lilly thought that the dog's barking took on a frantic quality; it sounded shriller than normal. Lilly raised her right hand up to shade her eyes from the sun, which was climbing the sky toward noon. She peered into the shade of her shack, and saw that the dogs had something under the floor and between the stilts it was built upon. They were taking turns shaking it and jumping back, yelping in their excitement.

"It's a snake, Momma; those dogs got themselves a snake!" James's eyes were almost wild with excitement and he briefly stopped in his tracks, but then he jumped up and down, with his arms flapping at his side. Suddenly, he was off in a flash.

"James!" Beth called after him. But her words were wasted on him. Beth shot an alarmed look at Grandpa.

Grandpa bellowed out, "James! Freeze boy; right there in your tracks!" James slid to a halt and looked back, exasperated.

"But, Grandpa, it might get away."

"Just hold onto your horses. You don't back talk your elders," Grandpa said gruffly.

Lilly gasped and clasped her fingers lightly over her lips and quickened her pace, gaining ground on Robert; instinctively.

"Fetch up that one next to you, Lilly," Beth said. Lilly breathlessly nodded her head.

"It's a rattler! It's a rattler!" James exclaimed to anyone who would listen. They all heard him because all of them were fixated on the scene before them.

Lilly had taken a hold of Robert by the back of his shirt. He pulled forward. "Careful or you're going to choke yourself," she told him.

"It's a rattler, Lilly," Robert said, nearly panting.

They drew closer to the shack and halted at a healthy distance from the dogs. "Those dogs are going to get bitten," Lilly said, unable to hide her anxiety. Just then the red hound shook the snake savagely and flung it. Before the snake could coil itself, the Blue Healer pounced upon it.

"Get back here, Blue!" Grandpa shouted at the dog. Blue shook the snake until his own muscled body shook in the frenzy. He paid no heed to Grandpa's command and shook the snake some more. The snake lashed out at the side of Blue's face with its fangs, but it could not quite reach. Blue flung the snake and both women screamed at the same instant.

"Who's afraid of a little old snake?" James said, puffing out his chest. Just then the red hound grabbed the snake and flung it right at James. The snake wrapped around one of the legs of his overalls and James eyes grew just about the size of saucers when he craned his head to look down. With the speed of greased lightning he shed his overalls. He did this so quickly that the adults didn't have a chance to pick up their chins off the desert floor from the first initial shock.

Grandpa was the quickest to move into action. "My God, see if he's been bitten!" Grandpa rushed over to the wood pile and grabbed a long stick and began to swing it at the dogs to keep them away from the snake.

James ran screaming and crying to Beth. Beth caught him in her arms and immediately began stripping the rest of his clothes off in a panic, screaming, "Where have you been bit? Where have you been bit?" James just continued to wail loudly. Tears and cries of terror contorted his face, while his mother franticly searched his little body.

Lilly, who was keeping Robert back away from the snake called to Grandpa, "Grandpa, you watch him, she needs some help." Lilly rushed up to James and took him firmly by the shoulders and shook him as hard as she dared. Kneeling so they were at eye level, she screamed right into his face, "Where did it bite you?"

"I don't know," he sobbed.

"Did it bite you?"

"I don't know, I don't think so," he cried a little less loudly now. Beth and Lilly exchanged quick glances and Lilly joined Beth in her search for bite marks.

"It would be swelling by now," Grandpa called out to the two women from his double post of watching Robert and wielding his stick at the dogs. Robert stood quietly, as if tranquilized, with his gaze transfixed on the pair of overalls lying in a heap upon the desert floor. There was no sound from the heap, but he knew what was there.

"I don't see anything, Beth," Lilly said.

"I don't see anything either," Beth said smiling at Lilly, and wrapped her arms around James, who was crying softly now. It was Beth's turn to cry. Happy tears of relief welled up in her eyes and gently flowed down her face as she squeezed James closer to her. Her tears became a soft rainfall upon his bare little shoulder. Lilly reached out and encircled the pair of them with her arms, pulling them close to her.

Grandpa smiled and silently thanked God for just one more miracle in his life. "If you girls are through being all mushy, I've got the business of this snake to tend too." Lilly patted James and bestowed a kiss upon one of his tear streaked cheeks and went over to relieve Grandpa of Robert. "You think it's still there?"

"Yeah, I sure do," he said while walking toward the heap of overalls, swinging the stick at the dogs and shouting, "Get back. Get out of here."

Lilly whistled and slapped her legs, "Here, Blue. Here, Jake. Tex, get over here!" She whistled again. Only Blue and Jake obeyed. Tex, the red hound, eyed her wily and slunk in a wide circle around Grandpa and made another dive toward the overalls. Grandpa caught him in the chest with his stick and shouted, "No! You darn good for nothing hound!" Tex yelped and stayed a respectable distance away from the old man after that.

"Grandpa, you be careful. Watch yourself, you hear?" Lilly called out after him.

"Child, I've been taking care of rattlers since before I could walk; just a baby sitting on my mommy's knee."

Beth led James by the hand over to where Lilly stood with Robert. "Cocky old thing isn't he?"

Lilly smiled and shook her head, "You can say that again."

Gingerly, Grandpa hooked one of the shoulder straps with his stick and slowly lifted it up. Robert nudged up next to Lilly and she bent down and picked him up. Grandpa gently shook the overalls and the snake fell free and squirmed back and forth upon the sand. Grandpa let the overalls slide off the stick and poked at the snake. It continued to writhe upon the ground, but did not coil. "That explains it. It sure does," Grandpa said.

"Explains what, Grandpa?" Lilly asked.

"It's dead. That explains why it didn't bite James. The dogs killed it."

"But why is it still moving?" James asked in a quivering small voice. He eyed the snake apprehensively.

"That's just its nerves making it do that." Grandpa said. "You're still lucky it didn't bite you though, because I've heard that they can."

Robert spoke up for the first time since the ordeal started. "Did any of the dogs get bit, Grandpa? Are they going to die?"

"I don't know son. I'll check them just as soon as I get this snake out of here. Now would you go fetch that yellow bucket, the one with the lid off of my front stoop for me?"

Robert looked at the snake and over at his mommy with those wide chocolate eyes of his. Lilly put Robert down and Beth leaned over and gave him a soft nudge, "Go on, go help Grandpa."

"I am not going to hold that bucket, Grandpa, while you put that old snake in there."

"Nobody's asking you to hold it; just go fetch it for me. Now hurry up, boy," Grandpa said, swinging at Tex again, but missing this time.

"Now get! Do as you were asked," Beth said firmly. Reluctantly, Robert obeyed. He climbed the rickety stairs that led up to Grandpa's porch and rummaged through the confusion of objects piled in the corner until he found the bucket which most closely matched Grandpa's description. Robert didn't bother with the stairs; he just tossed the bucket off the porch and leapt to the ground after it. Beth saw him do this and rolled her eyes skyward, while simultaneously sighing with relief.

Lilly smiled and shrugged, "I know they're going to break their legs doing that someday."

Robert ran past them, but stopped a respectful distance from Grandpa. "Is this the one, Grandpa?"

"Yep, that'll do her." Robert set the bucket down and joined the others.

All of them watched Grandpa skillfully pin the rattler's head beneath his stick. He dug into his pants pocket and withdrew his knife with his free hand. Robert held his breath momentarily and watched in total awe as Grandpa knelt down beside the snake and placed his knife blade over the back of its head. Both women turned their heads away at the same time but the two boys took a step closer and stared in fascination. "Yuck," Robert said, as Grandpa began sawing its head off.

"Beth, I need to borrow Buster's shovel to bury this head. His shovel is a might newer and sharper than that one of mine."

"Sure, Grandpa, I'll get it."

The others continued to watch Grandpa while Beth went off to get the shovel. Grandpa scooped the stick under the rattler's belly. The snake dangled limply on the stick for a few seconds and then it started to squirm again. "It's a big one, isn't it? And look at its pretty pattern." Grandpa tilted the stick over the bucket and let the snake slide in. Then Grandpa clamped the lid down on it.

"There isn't anything pretty about that darn old snake." Beth had returned with the shovel and handed it to Grandpa. Beth's voice was even and strong but Lilly saw her body shudder. Lilly herself felt weak in the knees and her gut was in a knot. It was over but that had been too close. Lilly looked at James and smiled and said in a light teasing manner, "You need some more overalls." James looked down at his shorts and bare legs, blushing instantly. James took off making a beeline for his cabin. He was back in a flash, with his clean overalls hooked only on one side.

"We had better get back to picking before this sun goes down," Beth said.

"Yeah, I reckon you're right, Beth. Let's go," Lilly said.

"I'll be along in a bit, girls; after I take care of this here business at hand."

"That'll be along about sundown," Beth said to Lilly, but loud enough so that Grandpa could overhear. Grandpa let the comment slide and headed in the direction of his shack. The sun had sunken lower on the western horizon when they returned to the field. They found Johnny asleep where they had left him.

"When is Johnny going to get up, Lilly? We want to tell him about the snake," Robert said.

"Yeah, he missed it," James added excitedly.

16

"Well, you sure didn't. Did you?" Beth chided him and playfully roughed up his hair. "Now scoot and don't bother Johnny. He's had enough of you two for one day."

Beth and Lilly went back to picking the cotton. The two boys played chasing each other through the rows of cotton for a bit until they grew tired and went back to the camp to watch Grandpa.

Dusk was spreading across the desert when Johnny stirred on the cot. He was thirsty. He sat up and ran his tongue over his dry lips, searching the fields for any sign of his mother. He spotted her toward the east end of the field closest to the shacks, stooping over a cotton bush next to Beth. He stood up and ambled over to her and said, "Mommy, I'm so thirsty."

Lilly smiled, "Well, Grandpa's got just the cure for that."

"He does?" Johnny asked in surprise.

"Yep, while you were sleeping, he brought us a little surprise."

Johnny's eyes lit up hopefully, "Soda pop?"

"Nope, better; lemonade, made from real lemons."

"Oh, that is not better then soda pop!"

"Come on, I'll get you some. We're mighty lucky to have that out here, son."

"Lilly, what do you say that we call it a day?" Beth asked.

Lilly glanced at the sun's position on the horizon and nodded. "That sounds good to me Beth. Would you like some more of this lemonade?"

"No, you guys go on ahead. I'm going to head on back and check on those two youngsters of mine."

"Beth, that was frightening today."

"It sure was."

"What was frightening, Mommy?" Johnny asked.

"I think I'll wait and let James tell you about it. He had quite an adventure today while you were napping."

Beth walked over to the bins with Johnny and Lilly. "I can't wait to get this sack off me, Lilly. By the end of every day, I feel like my spine is just going to crumble and that's going to be that."

Lilly replied, "I know, and it doesn't matter which shoulder you shift it to. They both hurt just the same. Someday I'm going to find an easier way to make a living."

"Well, when you do, look me up."

Beth and Lilly dumped their cotton into each of their own bins. "I'll see you back at the camp, Lilly."

Lilly said to Johnny, "Go get your cup."

"Finally, I thought I was going to get so thirsty I was going to die of it."

Lilly shook her head in bewilderment and said, "Just get the cup will you." Lilly peered into the bucket. The ice had melted. She reached down and felt the side of the bucket with her free hand. It still felt cool to the touch. She picked up the ladle and gave it a good stir. Johnny came over with the cup and watched the lemons floating on top whirl around the ladle. Eagerly, he pushed his cup at Lilly. "Well, hold it still and I'll give you some." Johnny held his cup over the bucket and Lilly filled it. He raised it to his parched lips and gulped it down, not wasting a drop. Lilly had to smile. He held his cup out to her again. Lilly lifted up one end of the bucket because the lemonade was almost gone, "This is your last cup." She filled his cup and then sat down on the cot to rest for awhile. The shade felt incredibly good to her.

"I want to go play with the boys, Mom." Johnny said.

"Well, you're just going to have to wait for awhile. I'm tired."

"Oh, how long?" he whined.

18

"Just give me a few minutes."

Johnny found a stick and occupied himself with drawing in the sand. Finally, Lilly got up and then they headed back to the shacks. When they got closer, Johnny could see Beth and Grandpa standing next to Grandpa's cauldron which he had hanging over the huge open fire pit, and the aroma of chili beans wafted towards him.

James raced toward Johnny and Lilly the moment he caught sight of them. "Look here Johnny; look at what I've got." James was shaking something next to his ear as he ran toward them. "Grandpa gave it to me."

Johnny ran to meet him. "What is it, James?"

"It's a rattler tail."

"Not really?"

"Yep, it sure is. Here listen for yourself." James shook it next to Johnny's ear.

"Lucky! Let me see it." Johnny reached for it.

James drew back his hand and put it behind his back. "Nope, only I touch this baby," he said quite smugly.

"Ah, let me see it!"

"Nope, it's mine!"

"I know that! I just want to see it."

"Okay, but I'm going to hold it." James stretched his arm out in front of him and opened his fingers; palm up to reveal his hidden treasure. Exhaling a large burst of air, Johnny's eyes almost bulged when he looked at the largest rattler tail he had ever seen.

"Fine, isn't it?"

"Oh my, I'll say," Johnny said with his eyes still riveted to the object of beauty on James's palm. "Where did Grandpa find it?"

"It found me. That's where he found it."

"What do you mean?"

"I meant just what I said. It found me. It wrapped itself right around the leg of my overalls with me in them."

"No!"

"Well, if you don't believe me, go ask Grandpa yourself!"

"You didn't get bitten?"

"Nope, I thought I did, but I didn't. And wait until you see what Grandpa's got."

"What, what is it?"

James waved one of his arms toward the shacks, "Come on, I'll show you."

Johnny followed James. Up ahead, Johnny could see Grandpa had a big flat square board propped up but he couldn't see the other side because it was facing the sun. When the two boys walked around to the front of it, what Johnny saw caused him to suck his breath in sharply. It was the biggest and most beautiful snake skin he had ever seen. "Wow! That's the loveliest thing I've ever seen in my whole life."

"You bet it is," Robert said as he walked up and overheard their conversation and threw in his own opinion. "And Grandpa's going to make himself a mighty fine belt out of it."

Johnny reached up and gingerly ran a finger along the silky pattern. He was afraid of snakes but this was a dead one, so he could touch it and he liked touching it. Even though he was afraid of them, he still thought they were sort of neat. He opened his hand and ran his whole hand up and down the length of the skin. Then the other two boys, one on either side of him, crowded in and took up his lead. They all had faint smiles of satisfaction on their youthful faces.

Beth said to Lilly, "Grandpa's gone and wrecked a perfectly good pot of chili beans. He put that old snake in there!"

Grandpa said, "Now Beth, I told you that it tastes just like chicken, only better. Isn't that so, Lilly?"

"Well, I don't know. I've never tasted it myself, but that's what I hear tell."

"Are you going to eat it, Lilly?" Beth asked.

"No, I don't think so, but I think I might have some of the beans."

"Now go on Beth and be a good girl and fry me up some of that Indian bread that I like to sop up my bean juice with."

"Oh, I reckon I will," Beth said.

The boys all came over to the pot and peered in. "What's for dinner?" Johnny asked.

"Beans and snake," Robert volunteered proudly.

"You sound as though you caught the thing yourself!" James chided.

"Well, you didn't catch it. It caught you!" Robert retorted and Johnny and Robert hugged each other in fits of laughter.

"I'll get you for that, Robert!" James said as he started toward the other two boys.

Beth who had been watching the boys reached out and grabbed James from behind by his overall straps. "Oh, no you won't, buster!"

"That's not my name; it's Dad's!"

"You get smart with me and you'll be the first one to get your tail end tanned with Grandpa's new belt."

"I'll fix some potatoes, Beth, to go with supper."

"That will be good, Lilly." Beth said, letting go of James.

"You tell them to stop poking fun at me!"

"You heard him, boys."

"Yes ma." Robert said.

"Johnny!" Lilly said.

"But, Mom, I wasn't making fun of him."

"You were laughing, that's the same thing."

"Yes, Momma," Johnny replied.

Lilly and Beth headed toward their respective shacks to gather the items they needed for dinner. When Lilly approached hers she noticed the door was slightly ajar. She thought, 'That's odd, I thought I closed that when I left this morning.' She swung the door open and there standing straddle-legged over her potatoes was Rex. He looked up at her with idle interest as his goatee on the bottom of his chin moved back and forth while he munched her potatoes. He calmly reached down for another bite. Lilly blew up and shouted, "You dang goat, get out of my potatoes!" She rushed over and grabbed her broom and landed a good blow to Rex's buttocks. This got his attention and he ran slipping and sliding on the old plank floor and out of the door with Lilly in hot pursuit. Rex took the quickest route that he could and leapt from the little porch to the ground. "Grandpa, you catch your dang old goat! He ate up my potatoes! I don't have any for our supper now."

"Rex is loose! Run for cover!" Robert shouted, and all three of the boys scattered. However, Rex paid them no mind and headed for cover himself, because he was intent on getting away from the broom-wielding Lilly.

Beth came out of her shack, carrying a heavy black cast iron frying pan and flour. "I have some potatoes, Lilly. You can use them, but we really ought to be boiling us up some old billy goat with them there beans instead of that snake."

"I don't think I'd eat that either," Lilly replied, and both women laughed.

Grandpa acted like he was nonchalantly walking past Rex and then snaked out his hand and grabbed Rex by his collar. Rex's bell jiggled loudly as he struggled to free himself from Grandpa's grip. "Why, this here goat is the finest billy on this side of the Mississippi. Without him you wouldn't have all those nannies kidding all the time. It's because of him you've got milk and cheese for your younglings and meat sometimes."

"Ah, any one of his offspring could fill the bill and you know it." Beth said. "He's old and ornery, just like you. That's why you two get along so famously."

"You better get to frying up that bread, woman! These here beans are nearly done."

Beth shook her head. "See what I mean. He's mean and ornery just like that goat. Come on Lilly, I'll get you those potatoes."

The two women headed toward Beth's shack together and Grandpa dragged Rex toward his tying post. Rex dug his hind legs into the ground and lunged sideways, resisting every step of the way.

Grandpa came back over to his beans, gave them a stir and ladled some of the broth out. He blew on it to cool it down before he took a sip. He frowned and dipped the ladle back in. He then reached over and picked up his fire poker. It was his special stick that he reserved for this purpose alone, except for an occasional swing at the dogs. Everyone knew that they had best not burn his fire poker. He used it to scoop out some of the coals from the fire into a heavy iron bucket. He carried those over to another fire pit, a smaller one with a grate. He swung the grate back with his foot and dumped the coals inside. He returned to the main fire, refilling his bucket several more times until there was a high bed of coals almost reaching up to the grate itself for the two women to cook upon.

Lilly peeled and sliced up her potatoes while Beth mixed the batter. The three boys were over by Rex playing like children do, chasing waves. When Rex would lunge at them they would run. But when he got closer to his post they crept toward him, but never too close. They would all giggle nervously as they crept in and screamed at the top of their lungs when he would charge, hitting the end of his

23

rope. "Someday, one of you is going to fall and that goat is going to get you." Beth called out to the boys. The boys paid her no attention and went on about their play.

"You're right about that, Beth. But I doubt that'll stop them for long," Lilly said.

"Yeah, I suppose you're right," Beth said, while watching Lilly place her skillet onto the grate.

"I want you two girls to come over here and tell me if my beans need some more chili," Grandpa said, dipping the ladle into his beans again.

Lilly took the ladle from him, blew softly and took a small sip. "I think just a little more, Grandpa, or else if you make them too spicy most of the kids won't eat them. What do you think, Beth?" Lilly asked as she passed the ladle over to Beth.

Beth tasted the beans and shook her head in agreement. "Yep, I think Lilly's right and maybe just a pinch more of salt."

The smell of the Indian bread frying drifted over to the boys and they let Rex be and all piled in line in front of Beth with their plates. Beth couldn't help but to smile at the eager, young faces all in a row. "You all go wash up and you get back in line the same way you left it." The two older boys raced over to the wash bucket but Johnny stood with his gaze riveted to the frying pan, as he watched in amazement as the bread bubbled up. Beth gave Johnny a gentle nudge and said, "Go on now, you too."

"Yes, Aunty Beth," he said, and then he turned and scampered after the other boys. When Johnny returned, Lilly sat him down at the big wooden plank table that Grandpa had made for these outside meals that they all loved to share. Then, Lilly sat his bowl of beans down in front of him and his cup of water. "Where's my bread, Momma?"

"It's got to cool a bit and then you can have it," Lilly said as she served up the other boys while Beth continued frying the bread. Lilly was just about to fill her own bowl when she heard Grandpa say, "I'll be darned!" Lilly looked up at him and his eyes were fixed on the road. Lilly turned to follow his gaze. There was an unfamiliar car coming up the dirt road towards them, with a billow of dust pluming out from behind it. The sun reflected off the windshield with a nearly blinding brilliance.

Chapter 3

The brand new 1957 two-tone blue and white Ford sedan pulled up to a stop about fifteen yards away from them. "I don't know anybody with a car like that," Beth said.

"I have a pretty good idea who it is," Grandpa said. Just then the driver's door opened and a tall young man with a slender build and a big cowboy hat stepped out. "Yep," Grandpa said.

"Howdy," the handsome stranger said as he walked up to them and extended his right hand out to Grandpa. Grandpa shook it and asked, "What the heck brings a rodeo star like you to these parts?"

"It's good to see you, old man." The young man said, ignoring Grandpa's question and openly eyeing Lilly up and down. "I'd have been here sooner; if I'd known the scenery had improved like it has."

"Yeah, I bet you would have!" Grandpa said.

Lilly felt uncomfortable under the stranger's gaze, so she filled her bowl, took it over to the table and sat down next to Johnny. Beth brought her over a piece of bread. Lilly smiled weakly and uttered her thanks to Beth.

"I thought I'd stop by the house and see Mom since I was passing through."

"It would have been nice if you could have seen your dad before he died; you know he was calling for you near the end."

"Yeah, I know; that was too bad, but you know I was in the middle of the championships when Mom called."

"We were just having some supper; would you like to sit down and have a bite with us?" Grandpa asked.

"Thanks but I just had Mom fix me a little something. But I'll sit awhile with you if these pretty ladies don't mind."

"Suit yourself," Grandpa replied.

He swung a long lanky leg over the bench, straddling the bench across the table from Lilly. He smiled at her and said, "Well, heck Grandpa, maybe you need to introduce me to these ladies?"

"They know who you are by now," Grandpa said.

James scraped up the last bit of beans from his plate and sopped up the juice with his bread. "Can I have some more of that snake, Mama?"

"You sure can, because I'm not going to eat any of it," Beth said, as she got up from the table, took his plate and walked over to the big cauldron. "But I must say the beans sure are good, Grandpa."

"Why, sure they are! That snake gave them a right nice flavor, if I do say so myself."

Beth smiled at the old man, "And so you do, just like you brag about everything else."

Leonard smiled across the table at Grandpa. "You really put a snake in those beans?"

"I did."

"I know you always said you were going to if you caught a big one."

"Yep, and I'm going to make myself a belt out of him too."

James got up from his seat and straddled the bench in front of Leonard facing him. "Are you really a rodeo champion?"

"Yep, I sure am."

"What's it like riding those wild horses?"

27

"I don't ride the horses, they're for sissies. I ride the bulls. The Brahmas would just as soon kill you as look at you."

James's eyes were about the size of saucers. "Wow, aren't you scared when you get on them?"

"Darn tootin', I'm scared, but that's what makes it fun."

"That doesn't make any sense to me. When I'm scared, I'm scared; I wouldn't get on one of them," James said.

"I wouldn't either!" Johnny exclaimed.

"I'd do it!" Robert said, smugly. "I'd just stare that old bull right in the eye, and then I'd spit in it and climb right aboard."

"You wouldn't either. No sir, you'd be too afraid to get onto an old dumb horse," James said.

Beth brought the plate back to the table and sat it down where James had been seated. "James, you get back over here and eat, and I want both of you two boys to hush up. There isn't anyone in my family that's going to be riding bucking bulls, or horses for that matter."

"That's exactly what my mother said when she found out that I was going to start riding in the rodeos," Leonard said. Leonard winked at James and James smiled in return. Beth glared at Leonard, but he pretended not to notice.

"You women go ahead and clear up the dishes and Leonard and I will amble on over to the patch and turn on the irrigation pipes; it's cool enough now."

"You go ahead and take your time, Lilly and I will manage just fine." Beth then turned to Lilly and asked, "Would you like any more of the beans, Lilly, or maybe Johnny would?"

"Not me, Beth, thanks. How about you Johnny?

Johnny shook his head no and said, "I want Grandpa to tell me a story though."

"I do too!" Robert said

"Yeah," added James.

"I don't know about tonight; he has company," Lilly said.

Beth turned toward the boys. "You all go fetch me some water for these dishes."

"Oh, Mom," James whined, "they always make me carry most of it. They should have to do it this time; all by themselves."

"You are the biggest, that's why. Now go on and stop your belly aching!" Beth handed them each a metal bucket. "Hurry up so we can get these dishes washed."

"Last one to the well is a rotten egg," Johnny yelled, and then he dashed ahead of the older two. They didn't seem to notice Johnny's advantage and headed out behind him in hot pursuit. Dust flew up behind them and drifted toward the two women.

Beth tried to fan the dust away from her face with her hand and said, "I sure do wish I had just a quarter of the energy that these kids have. Lilly, imagine the cotton we could pick with that."

Lilly laughed and Beth joined her. "We'd have this whole field wiped out in two days. And then maybe we could go on to Fort Bragg and just sit in that cool ocean breeze," Lilly said.

"That sounds good to me," Beth responded. "What do you want to put these left-over beans in?"

"We should put them in one of Grandpa's bowls. He'll want to have them for dinner tomorrow, don't you think?"

"Yep, I'll go get one." Beth went to get the bowl from Grandpa's shack, while Lilly scraped the dishes. Beth came back and handed Lilly the bowl. Beth then said to Lilly, "What do you think is taking those boys so long?"

"They're tossing stones in the well, most likely."

Even with Johnny's advantage of the head start, James had reached the well first and Robert was second. "Rotten egg," James yelled at Johnny. "You're the rotten egg!"

"I don't care," Johnny lied, "not one little bit."

"Let's get some stones," Robert interrupted, "let's see how long it takes them to drop today." The boys fanned out around the well, each heading in a different direction, and stooped low to the ground to pick the best of the stones from those scattered about their feet.

Johnny was just about to pick up a great dropping stone that was rounded smooth and flat on both sides like a small pancake, which would make a fantastic plop, when his eyes lit up and his heart quickened its pace. He froze just as he was hovering almost directly over the most beautiful specimen of the horned toad species that he had ever seen. The toad rotated its eyes upward in its sockets as it was watching Johnny. Johnny knew that his only hope of catching it was to anticipate which direction that it would head in and, if he was wrong, his prize would be forever lost to the desert. He longed to call out for the other two boys to elicit their help, but he knew that a sudden noise would startle the reptile. He was on his own. He sucked his breath in slowly and held it. He wanted this lizard more than anything else he could think of at the moment. It was a beauty; there was just no doubt about it. Johnny slowly began to bend lower, ever so slowly; he was hoping that the lizard wouldn't notice, but it did. The horned toad made a run for cover and Johnny sprang for it with the quickness of a cougar. Johnny felt it squirming beneath his hands and sweet joy washed over his whole body and swelled within his heart. He could not remember when he had been so happy.

The other two boys came over to see what all the commotion was about. Johnny was lying flat on his tummy, still on the ground with his arms stretched out in front of him. Robert peered down at Johnny inquisitively and said, "You aren't having one of those fits I've heard about are you?"

Johnny rolled over onto his back and held his catch up in the air with both hands, triumphantly. He was grinning from ear to ear. Robert stepped closer to investigate and then, when the realization of what Johnny held in his hands hit him, he let out a whoop and literally jumped up and down with joy. James's mouth rounded into a perfect circle like the letter O and his eyes widened to match. Johnny carefully sat up and proudly said, "Isn't it something?"

"Let me hold it," Robert said, reaching for the lizard in Johnny's hand.

"He is mine! I found him," Johnny said, drawing his lizard protectively closer to his chest.

"Ah, come on; I just want to see him for one minute," Robert pleaded.

"Nope," Johnny said, shaking his head stubbornly and holding his ground.

"Let me hold him," James asked wistfully.

"I'm not going to let anybody hold him because he might get away."

"Where are you going to keep him?" James asked.

"I haven't thought about it yet."

"Well, you could put him in one of these buckets for right now and then we could all get a good look at him," James volunteered.

"Yeah, that's a great idea James, but you'll have to carry more water because there isn't going to be anybody carrying my horned toad but me."

"If I have to carry the most water again, then I get to draw it."

"Suit yourself," Robert said, "we don't care about drawing any old water. We've got ourselves a horned toad here."

"Yeah, you go ahead and suit yourself," Johnny said, as he got up off the ground and walked over to one of the buckets where he gently deposited his lizard. He watched it closely while it tried to jump up on the sides of the bucket to escape, but to no avail. It

31

slipped back into the bottom of the bucket each time it tried. All three of the boys huddled around the bucket with their eyes riveted on the little reptile captured within.

"What have you all got yourselves in that bucket?" All three of the boys looked up at the same time. Grandpa was walking toward them with Leonard. It was Grandpa who had spoken.

Robert broke free of the huddle and ran up next to Grandpa. Tugging on Grandpa's arm, Robert exuberantly exclaimed, "Johnny's caught himself a horned toad, Grandpa! Come on, I'll show it to you."

"Now hold on, I'm coming, boy. You don't have to drag me." Grandpa allowed Robert to lead him over to the bucket and Leonard followed.

"Why, I haven't seen a horned toad in years," Leonard said smiling brightly.

"See all the excitement you've been missing in these parts since you've left, Leonard." Grandpa winked at the younger man.

Leonard smiled at Grandpa with only one side of his mouth. "Yeah, I can see that, Grandpa."

Grandpa leaned over the bucket to take a look at the lizard. "Why, that's the finest horned toad I ever did see. What do you think, Leonard?"

"I must say she sure is mighty fine."

Grandpa looked up and saw that Leonard was no longer looking at the lizard and followed Leonard's gaze. Lilly was approaching them; her simple cotton dress billowing behind her as she walked toward them into the slight breeze that skirted just above the desert floor. She looked eloquent, but Lilly was just that way. A lot of women could dress up in fancy gowns and pearls and have their hair piled high on their heads, and they still couldn't look like Lilly in her simple cotton dress.

"It is fine, isn't it, Grandpa?" Johnny asked, seeking the old man's approval.

"Why, of course it is fine, I've done said it was, but I'll say so again. It's fine. The finest on this here desert, I do declare!" Grandpa said affectionately, while roughing up Johnny's hair.

Lilly drew closer. "You boys are supposed to be bringing us dishwater."

"Oh, they stumbled upon something much more important than mere dishwater, Lilly," Grandpa said.

"What might that be, Grandpa?"

Johnny got up and ran over to his mother, "Mom, I got myself the best horned toad in all the land. Grandpa even said so."

"Oh, he did? And you do. You've got yourself a lizard?"

"Not just a lizard, Mommy, it's a horned toad. It's the best."

"Well, I don't know anything about the best kind of lizards, but I do know one thing, you're not going to be keeping it!"

Johnny's face fell and his chin began to quiver. He looked at his mother with astonished disbelief as tears stung and welled in his eyes.

"Oh, Lilly, what's wrong with this here little old lizard?" Grandpa asked.

"It's a horned toad, Grandpa," Johnny interjected. Grandpa looked at Johnny and saw the first tear spill over the brim of his lower lid. It streaked down his right cheek and left a bright shiny path where it had cleaned away the dust in its path.

"It's a reptile, they give me the creeps."

Grandpa said, "You've got to be a male, Lilly, to have appreciation for these things."

Lilly responded, "Well then, thank God for that."

"Look at that boy, Lilly. You've got to have a heart."

Lilly looked at Johnny and her face softened. "Where are we going to keep it, Grandpa? We can't keep it in that bucket."

"Heck no, Lilly, I've got an old crate over there by the side of my shack. I can fix something out of that."

Johnny's face brightened. "You're going to let me keep it, Mommy?"

Lilly faked a frown. "I suppose so."

Johnny ran over to her and hugged her. "I just knew you couldn't be so mean."

"Oh, I can be so mean, but it's just Grandpa can be more persuasive than I can be mean."

Leonard said, "We can always count on Grandpa to save the day."

Grandpa said, "That you can. Well, we had best be heading back or Beth will be after all of us. And there is no worse fate than the wrath of Beth."

Lilly smiled at his humor, "I'll tell her you said that. She'll take it as a compliment."

James got up and began to draw the water from the well. "Go ahead and fill them up all the way, James," Lilly said. "We're one bucket short seeing how this lizard seems to be taking up temporary residence in this one."

James whined, "I can't carry one so full, Lilly."

"I know these two gentlemen would be pleased to carry them for you," Lilly said, as she smiled at Grandpa and Leonard.

James filled the buckets and they all headed back toward the camp together. When they drew nearer, Robert ran ahead so he could be the first one to tell his mother about the lizard. Johnny took it up to Beth so she could have a good look at it.

"Tell me you're not going to put that lizard in the beans the next time you make them, are you Grandpa?" Beth asked.

Johnny looked at Grandpa horrified. "No, I wouldn't do that to the boy's horned toad. Don't you fret Johnny; your reptile is safe with me."

The men poured the water into the cauldron and Beth stoked up the fire with a couple pieces of wood.

"Well, I guess I had better fix that horned toad a proper dwelling," said Grandpa. "Beth, do you think Buster would mind if I helped myself to a little of that wire mesh of his?"

"No, I don't reckon he would; especially since it is for such a noble cause."

"As a matter of fact, you're darn tootin' it is," Grandpa replied.

"Johnny, what are you going to call your horned toad?" Leonard asked.

"I'm going to call him King! Grandpa said he is going to live in a noble dwelling and since he is the best reptile around, it just makes sense to call him King."

"That sounds good to me!" Grandpa volunteered.

"I think you ought to give it some more thought!" Robert said.

"Nope, I don't need too! King is a great name for a great reptile. He's king of the desert. That's him!"

"Well, come on guys; let's go make us a reptilian castle, what do you say?" Grandpa asked.

"Do I get to hammer?" James wanted to know.

"Sure, you can all hammer," Grandpa answered

"I want to put on the door," Robert said.

"Not a problem!" Grandpa replied.

"Yeah let's go," Robert said. They all headed toward Grandpa's shack. Even Leonard, who looked back reluctantly at Lilly, followed.

When steam began to drift up off of the water in the pot, Beth took two pot holders and wrapped them around the tall thin handle. With a grunt, she gingerly hoisted the huge pot off the flame and carefully poured half of the water into the old rubber tub that doubled as wash basin and dish sink. She sat the pot down next to the tub on the end table.

Lilly walked up and poured some dish soap into the tub. She began stacking the dishes into the tub. Beth slung a dish towel over her shoulder. "I guess I'm drying, this time?"

"Yup, I guess so," Lilly said as she washed the dishes and piled them next to Beth's pot.

All of the guys had gathered in the shade of Beth's cabin where the wire was. "Look at them over there," Beth chuckled. "They all look like a bunch of little boys gathered around that reptile."

Grandpa said, "Robert, go fetch me that crate under my stairs, would you? And James would you mind bringing me my tool box and that saw? I'll get the wood. We've got to make a tray for the bottom to hold some sand."

"Yeah, that's a swell idea," James said, "lizards like sand."

"Why? Why do lizards like sand, James?" Johnny asked.

James looked at him and shrugged, "I don't know."

"They like to hide in it," Leonard said, "and it helps to keep them warm too."

"Oh, like a blanket," Johnny said. "I hide under my blanket when I get scared too."

"You're just a baby!" James said.

"I am not a baby!"

"Yes you are!"

"That will be enough!" Grandpa said gruffly.

Beth finished the dishes and carefully stacked them into three different piles. One pile belonged to Lilly, one to Grandpa, and the last one belonged to her. She took her stack of dishes and started to climb up the steps to her shack. She stopped to survey the construction project in progress. Both of the men and all three boys where huddled around the cage, deeply engaged in their undertakings. "I've never seen so much fuss over a dang lizard in all my days!" she said. They all looked up at her with bemused faces. Beth shook her head back and forth and said, "I didn't think you bunch would understand."

"Understand what?" Leonard asked on behalf of the group.

"How silly you all are for making such a fuss over a reptile."

James spoke up in defense of the group. "It's so cool, Mom! You don't understand us, because you're a girl." In unison they all nodded in agreement with James's statement.

"I can see I'm clearly outnumbered here. You boys just continue as you were," she said, and then continued on into her shack. She was smiling, proud of herself, because she had put special emphasis on the word 'boys'. She knew Grandpa would have caught that.

"It's my turn to hammer," Robert said, reaching to take the tool out of James's hand.

"My turn's not over yet," James said defensively, drawing the hammer closer to his chest and out of Robert's reach.

"It is Johnny's turn next," Grandpa said. "Both of you two have had turns. So, when you get finished with that nail, James, give the hammer to Johnny."

"Oh, alright," James said reluctantly.

"You had best move your fingers out of the way, boy," Leonard advised James. James looked up at Grandpa for reassurance, to see if Leonard was right.

"Go ahead," Grandpa said. "You've got that nail steady enough. Just come down on it straight from the top, so it won't bend on you. Tap it a couple of times, just to make sure your angle is right and then give it a good whack. Make sure your fingers are out of the way though." James followed the orders, being very careful to take their heed regarding his fingers. When he was finished, he very proudly handed Johnny the hammer.

"You're going to make a fine carpenter someday, James," Grandpa stated.

"What about me, Grandpa?" Robert demanded to know.

"You will too. You did a mighty fine job."

Johnny drove home the last couple of nails on the tray. All the boys watched intently while Grandpa crafted a swinging door on the old crate. Next Grandpa skillfully cut and bent the wire, and then tacked it in place inside the crate. Grandpa handed Johnny the tray and said, "Go fill it up with some sand and a couple of rocks that King can use for shade." Johnny took the tray and went in search of sand, which was everywhere, and the perfect rocks for shade. Following closely on his heels were his two playmates.

"I think it would be cool to build King a cave, so he could sleep in it if he wanted too," Robert said.

"I don't think lizards live in caves," James said authoritatively.

"They do so!" Robert said vehemently.

"I know," Johnny said, "we can build him a cave and see."

"I think that is a good idea," Robert said, shooting his older brother a victorious look.

"You guys go ahead and suit yourselves," James said smugly. He was careful not to show his disappointment at being defeated.

The three of them searched for the perfect stones, comparing and rejecting the imperfect specimens. They worked together until they were satisfied that they had found the only stones that would do. When they returned, Johnny slid the tray into place. Then, the other two boys handed Johnny the stones, one by one. Johnny set up the cave carefully, wedging the stones deep into the sand on top of the tray.

"We need something to put water in," James said. Looking around, he spied an old tuna fish can and scrambled up to get it. "Will this old can do? Maybe if we just dig it into the sand a bit. You know, to make it look like a natural drinking hole." He handed it to Johnny.

Johnny started to put it into the cage and then handed it back to James. "It needs some water in it."

"Oh, it sure does," he said, blushing slightly. He took it over to the water bucket and submerged it.

Beth walked up behind James just then and said, "Just what were you thinking when you put that dirty can into our drinking bucket?"

"King has to have some water, Momma."

"Well, who am I to question, if it is for the King. Next time use the ladle. That's what it is there for," she said, before playfully swatting him on the back of his head. He took the water back over to Johnny and handed it to him. Johnny worked it down into the sand so that the lip of the can was just above the surface of the sand.

Grandpa and Leonard now sat by the dying embers of the camp fire, and Beth looked down from her porch and said to her boys, "Come on you two, it's time to turn in for the night."

Robert protested. "Oh, Mom, we wanted to see if King will go inside his cave."

"That will just have to wait until tomorrow. Now come on you two." Beth's two boys reluctantly got up from the side of the cage and climbed the stairs.

"Goodnight Johnny," Robert said.

"Goodnight guys. We'll play with King tomorrow."

They went into their shack and Johnny could hear them stirring around inside, as he sat beside the cage and admired his new catch. He could barely see the outline of the lizard in the moonlight.

Lilly came out of her shack and walked down the steps and across to the table beside the fire pit. She picked up her stack of dishes that Beth had set aside for her earlier.

"Need some help with that, pretty lady?" Leonard asked.

"No." Lilly said flatly. "Johnny, come on, it's time for bed." Johnny gave King one more loving glance and got up to follow his mother up the steps.

Grandpa put a couple more logs onto the fire to stoke it up. He come back over to his chair and leaned back, burrowing deep into the soft cotton. He had made the cushion himself. It was just a couple of burlap sacks, stuffed with cotton and sewn together in the center. He sank deep enough into it that it helped to keep him warm. In no time at all he was snoring loudly.

Leonard looked over at Grandpa and smiled. He stood up and said to the sleeping man, "I guess I will see you next time I'm around you old fart." Come morning, Leonard was back on the road following the rodeos.

Chapter 4

When Johnny woke in the morning he could smell salt pork cooking. He knew Grandpa was making them a special breakfast. Johnny and Lilly got dressed and walked together to the campfire.

Beth stood beside Grandpa and Johnny heard Beth say, "Grandpa, if you put that darn snake in the pot with the salt pork and fried potatoes, you're not going to get any of my onions to go with it."

"Okay, okay, you win; just go fetch me an onion, and make it a big one." Beth shook her head in affirmation and then walked off to her cabin to get the onion.

Grandpa looked up from his pot when he saw Lilly approaching with Johnny. "Did you hear that?" He asked Lilly. "The sun has hardly crested the horizon and she's already picking on this poor old man."

"I don't know how Buster manages to survive her," Lilly said, mocking sympathy for him.

"Those were my thoughts exactly! When I was young, I could have handled a woman like that though. But throughout the years, women like that have taken a toll on me."

"You weren't really going to put the rest of that snake in there, were you?" Lilly asked.

Grandpa could see that Beth was approaching within hearing range of them. He winked at Lilly and said, "Sure, I was going to put that snake in there. I know Buster loves the flavor and since he didn't get any of it last night, I was just trying to be thoughtful, that's all."

"Buster is home now?"

"Yep, he pulled in late last night," Grandpa responded. Beth gave Grandpa a baleful look and handed him the onion.

Lilly asked, "Where are Buster and the boys?"

Beth said, "Off looking for a roommate for King. Can you believe it? They are actually lizard hunting. The two boys convinced their dad that King looked lonely."

Lilly asked, "How can you tell if a lizard is lonely?"

Beth shrugged her shoulders and said, "It beats the heck out of me."

"I know how you can tell," Grandpa chimed in. The two women looked at him quizzically. "Well, if you know that you have a boy lizard, he's going to be lonely unless you find him a girl lizard."

Beth rolled her eyes and said, "Lilly, we should have known that we wouldn't get a straight answer out of this one."

Lilly smiled and asked, "How far off is breakfast, Grandpa?"

"About fifteen minutes, give or take a few," he said.

Beth said, "I reckon that I had better go find those three lizard hunters, Lilly. I sure hope they don't find one. I hate reptiles."

"Well, naturally Beth. The reason that they like them is because they are boys. Girls have more sense."

The two women went to gather up their dishes and when they returned to the fire, they could see Buster and the two boys off in the distance. They were heading toward the camp.

"Isn't it just like a man to know when the food is ready?" Beth asked Lilly. Lilly smiled and nodded her head in agreement.

"You two women seem to do a mighty fine job of timing yourselves," Grandpa chided them.

Beth stepped up next to him and planted a kiss on one of Grandpa's cheeks and said, "That's only because no one can cook as good as you do."

"That's just like you to turn on the sugar when you get yourself into trouble," he told her.

"That's because it works every time. It sweetens you right up. And the Lord knows you can use it," Beth said. She smiled and then gently squeezed his arm affectionately. Lilly laughed at the antics of the two and began to scoop the food onto her plates.

The two boys ran up ahead of Buster to the fire. "That sure does smell good, Grandpa," Robert said.

"You must be hungry," Grandpa replied.

"We're starving," James spoke up, before Robert had a chance to reply.

"Where is your lizard?" Grandpa asked the two boys.

Robert swept one of his arms in the direction of the fields. "It's still out there hiding somewhere. But James and I fully intend to find it today."

Grandpa raised his brows and asked, "Oh, you do, do you?"

"You can hang your hat on that Grandpa," James said.

"Are you getting smart with your elders, young man?" Beth said, scolding him.

"Yes, Momma," James said. Beth glared at James and James quickly corrected himself. "I meant to say no, Momma."

"That is more like it," Beth retorted.

Buster walked up to the fire and said playfully to Grandpa, "Did I see you trying to steal my woman while I was gone?"

Grandpa replied, "She was the one doing all the kissing. I'd have a talk with her, if I were you. I can't help it if I'm so dang handsome. My daddy was a looker too."

"This here old sourpuss needed some sweetening up," Beth told Buster. "I'm glad that lizard is still out there hiding somewhere," she added.

"Don't say that, Momma, you're going to jinx us," Robert said.

Grandpa said, "Come on let's eat."

James and Robert climbed onto the bench across the table from Johnny and Lilly. James asked Johnny, "Can you help us look for lizards after breakfast, Johnny? You're really good at finding them."

"I sure can," he replied.

James swung his legs around to the side of the bench and away from the table, stood up and announced, "I'm going to check out how King is getting along in his new home."

"I'm coming with you," Robert said, and got up to follow his big brother.

"I'm coming too," Johnny said.

"You all may, after all of us finish our breakfast young men," Lilly told them firmly.

"Okay," Johnny muttered, and the disappointment showed upon his face.

"That lizard will still be there after all of you get done eating," Buster reassured them.

Finally, the boys were excused from the table, and sat down upon the sand next to the lizard's cage. The horned toad tried to bury itself deeper into the sand on the bottom of the cage, but the sand was not deep enough. "We are going to have to find King some bugs," James said.

Johnny asked the other two boys, "Do you think King has gone inside of his cave yet?"

"I don't know," Robert said.

James leaned over to have a closer look at the cage. "We can look for tracks, to see if he has gone in." When James leaned in toward the cage, this alarmed the horned toad and he flattened himself down on the bottom of the cage, and then he quickly, with surprising speed, made a dash for the cave. All the children could see of him was his tail sticking out one side.

A large grin swept across Johnny's face and he announced proudly, "He likes it."

"It will help keep him cool when the sun is straight up," Robert said.

"Come on, you guys, let's go look for our lizard, before it gets too hot," James said. All the children got up and followed James into the field at the edge of the camp.

"Where are they most likely to hide?" Robert asked Johnny.

"Under rocks," he replied.

The children fanned out in their search for a friend for King. By the end of the day there was still no friend for King found. And at the dinner table that evening Grandpa made an announcement that took them all by surprise. Grandpa said, "Lilly you did not know anything about this, but I took it upon myself to make an inquiry of a friend of mine. He owns a fine lodge in Fort Bragg and I received a letter from him today in response to my inquiry. He is willing to offer you a job as an apprentice to one of his chefs."

Lilly could not believe her ears. "Grandpa, I can't just up and leave all of you. All of you have grown to be like family to Johnny and I."

Grandpa reached across the table and took one of Lilly's hands and said, "You need to do this for both you and your boy. This is no life out here for a single woman, Lilly."

Beth said, "Lilly, Grandpa is right. God knows, we don't want to see you go. But this desert is no good for you. It is no good for any of us, Lilly. If we had a chance, we would be out of here as well."

Grandpa went on to say, "My friend, Lou, is willing to give you and Johnny room and board and then pay after you learn all of the ropes."

Johnny sat in stunned disbelief. He could not believe what he was hearing. He looked at the faces of his two friends and felt tears welling up in his eyes. James was the first one to speak up, "You don't have to take the job, Lilly. You already have a job right here."

Beth reached out and pulled her son to her, and said to him, "James, opportunities like this do not come around to people very often. Even though we don't want our friends to leave, we have to think what is really best for them."

Chapter 5

The three boys were uncharacteristically quiet while they ate their meal. James and Robert didn't even pick at one another. When they finished their meal, Lilly said, "Johnny, why don't you and your friends go and play fetch with the dogs."

"Yes ma'am," Johnny said, and he climbed down from his bench. Beth's two boys followed and they walked toward where the dogs were laying, just at the edge of the camp's firelight. The dogs got up with their tails wagging to come greet the three boys.

Robert picked up a stick and threw it out in front of the dogs. The whole pack of dogs went yelping after it. Blue was the victor. He was younger than the rest. The other dogs tried to latch onto the other end, but Blue ran back, dodging through the pack like a football player running to make a touchdown.

Blue stopped in front of Robert and dropped the stick. Robert bent over, picked it up and tossed it again. The dogs wheeled around in a tight pack and sprang after it. Tex lunged on top of the stick this time. Jake grabbed one end of the stick and tried to make off with it. Tex clasped his jaws down on the other end to hold onto his prize. The two dogs tugged on the stick, pulling against each other. Tex lowered his haunches and backed up, dragging Jake across the sand. Jake's legs were sprawled out as he tried to use his weight to hold his position, but he was no match for the much larger hound. The three boys laughed at the comical sight. It felt good for them to laugh. Johnny looked over at the campfire and saw that the four adults were deep in conversation. The glow of the firelight illuminated their faces.

Later that night Lilly put Johnny to bed and returned to the campfire. She sat there and listened as her friends encouraged her that this move to Fort Bragg, California was in the best interest of both her and Johnny.

When the evening wore to a close, Buster held a lantern and walked with the two women; Beth with an arm around Lilly's shoulder to Lilly's shack. The glow of a lantern that Lilly had already lit spilled out between the cracks. The three stopped at the base of the stairs. Lilly turned to face Beth and Buster and said, "Thank you for your kindness."

Beth affectionately squeezed Lilly's arm and said, "We will always be here for you, Lilly."

Then Lilly climbed the stairs and closed the door behind her. She turned to see that Johnny was already asleep. She could see the streaks upon his round little cheeks that his tears had made. He had apparently cried himself to sleep. She put on her slip that she slept in and blew out the lantern. She crawled under the covers and snuggled up next to Johnny. And soon she was fast asleep.

The next morning Lilly emerged from her cabin and poured a cup of coffee and sat down at the campfire across from Beth. Beth scooted to the edge of her chair and watched Lilly's face intently. Beth knew she wouldn't lose her friend. There would be distance between them, but they would always be friends. "Now that you have slept on it, how does it sound to you?" Beth asked Lilly.

Buster stoked the fire and left the two women alone to talk. He went to wake up his boys and then told them, "Go get Johnny up."

Robert sat up and rubbed the sleep from his eyes and asked, "Where is Lilly?"

"She is sitting at the fire with your momma," Buster said, and turned to get the plates for breakfast. "Oh, fetch their plates for them while you're in there too."

Robert reached over and shook James. "Wake up you sleepy head." James rolled over onto his side and threw his arm up over his face. Robert shook him again. James moaned and flung his arm from his face toward Robert. Robert leaned back just in the nick of time and grinned.

Buster turned back toward the boys with the dishes in his hand just in time to see it. "You're asking for it, Robert. He's going to get you and I don't want you to come crying to me or your momma."

Robert stood up on the bed and flung the covers back off his brother. "Rise and shine!" James sat up and grabbed for Robert. With lightning speed, Robert sprang off the bed and jumped behind his father.

Now that James was awake, Buster said again, "You two need to go fetch Johnny, because breakfast is almost ready." Buster climbed down the wooden steps and headed for the table.

Robert and James dressed and jumped from the top stoop and raced each other toward Johnny's shack. It wasn't long before all three of the boys were sitting at the table. James and Robert sat flanking Johnny on either side. Grandpa set a steaming plate of grits and salt pork down in front of Johnny. "Eat up my young man, so you can grow strong and handsome like Grandpa here."

Johnny smiled and said, "Thank you, Grandpa."

"You're not nearly as good looking as I am," Buster challenged.

With a twinkle in his eyes, Grandpa replied, "You just stroll over to that fire and ask those two women what they think."

Buster looked toward the fire where Beth was kneeling beside Lilly's chair and said, "I best not."

"See, I thought so," Grandpa said. "That settles it then."

Robert came to his father's defense. "You shouldn't give up so easy, Daddy. I think you're handsome. I'm going to look just like you when I grow up."

Buster sat a plate of food down in front of his two boys, reached across the table and roughed up Robert's hair and said, "Then that's all that counts to me." Robert gave his father a huge apple-cheeked smile.

Grandpa walked over to the fire and said, "Ladies, I've made grits this morning and you want to have some while they are fresh. They taste the best then."

"Coffee is good for me, Grandpa, thank you," Lilly said.

"Come on, Lilly. You've got to try to eat something. It's going to be a long day," Beth coaxed her.

"I made those grits just for you, Lilly. You know how stingy I usually am with my grits," Grandpa said, trying to encourage her.

Lilly caved in to her two well-meaning friends. "I reckon I will try. But not too much, Grandpa, I don't want to waste any."

"There is never anything that is a waste on you, Lilly," Grandpa replied.

Beth stood up, took Lilly by the hand and pulled Lilly up from her chair. "Come on, let's go have some breakfast." Beth walked over to the table with her arm around Lilly's shoulder and sat down beside her on the bench. Buster was ready with their plates and sat them down in front of the women. The two men served themselves up and slid onto the bench across the table from Lilly and Beth.

"This looks good, Grandpa, thank you." Beth said.

"Yes, thank you, Grandpa," Lilly said weakly.

"It is my pleasure, ladies."

The children finished their breakfast and headed off toward the field to play. The dogs scampered about their feet.

After breakfast Grandpa said, "I can watch after the boys if you ladies would like to ride into town with Buster, when he goes, if you need groceries."

"I would like that," Lilly said. She looked at Beth.

"I would like to go too," Beth replied. "Are you sure that you're up to watching all three of them, Grandpa?

"We'll all be just fine. You ladies just go ahead and go."

The two women climbed onto the front seat of the Ford, with Beth in the center next to Buster. Grandpa stood and watched them drive toward the highway. Shortly, all he could see was a plume of dust. He turned away and headed for the shade trees. He felt weary and he needed to rest. He would make a late supper so, when the three returned from town, they could have something warm to eat. He sat down in Beth's chair and from there he could see all the boys playing tag out in the field. That was good, because they would wear themselves out and be no trouble later. They might even want a nap. He smiled at that idea, because they would be no trouble at all. Heck, he might even be able to take a nap too. He looked beyond the boys at the standing fields of cotton. He closed his eyes and took a deep breath. When Grandpa opened his eyes again, the three boys where standing in front of him and Blue was licking his hand, startled, he realized that he must have drifted off to sleep.

"Where did Mom go?" Robert asked.

"She and Lilly rode into town with Buster, to get some more groceries."

Grandpa sat up straighter in his chair and said, "Hey, you guys, if the three of you come over to Mrs. Bailey's house with me and pull some weeds in her garden, I bet I can talk her out of some more lemons."

Robert's face brightened. "For some more lemonade?" he asked.

"You bet," Grandpa replied. "How about it Johnny; what do you think?"

Johnny shrugged his small shoulders and said, "Sure, why not."

Grandpa struggled out of the chair and said," Well then, let's get started, shall we?" He took Johnny's tiny hand and led the way, with the other two boys following silently behind.

Mrs. Bailey was out on her screened-in porch when she saw the four of them approaching. She opened the door and walked out into the yard to greet them. "What a pleasant surprise," she said warmly.

"These boys thought that maybe, if they pulled some weeds for you, we could get some more lemons," Grandpa said.

"Well, that is a very nice offer, but really it won't be at all necessary. The four of you just go right ahead and pick as many lemons as you like."

"That's right nice of you, Mrs. Bailey, but I know that you have a weed patch back there in your garden. You could use some help and we men like to earn our keep," Grandpa said.

"Those weeds aren't going anywhere; they will be just fine. Now you guys go ahead and get your lemons. I'll get the bucket with ice," she smiled warmly at them again, before turning toward the steps leading into her house.

James called out after her, "That's very nice of you, Mrs. Bailey; thank you."

She turned around and replied to him, "You are very welcome, sweetheart," and she continued on into her house.

James sprinted around the side of the house and was the first to shimmy up the lemon tree. He smiled down gleefully at the two younger boys that stopped at its base. Grandpa walked up to the tree and looked up at James. Grandpa shook his head, and couldn't help but smile. He stooped down and interlocked his fingers to form a cup. "Come on Johnny, put one of your feet here in my hands and I will give you a boost up." Johnny put one foot in Grandpa's hands and clung to Grandpa's shoulders for support. "Put your hands on the trunk of the tree and walk them up to steady yourself while I give you a lift." Johnny did as he was told and soon stepped onto the lower bough.

Smiling, Johnny looked down at Grandpa "Thanks Grandpa."

Grandpa simply nodded and said to Robert, "Come on, it's your turn now." Robert walked up to Grandpa and looked up hesitantly at the tree. "You'll be just fine," Grandpa said encouragingly. "Johnny move over and make plenty of room for Robert." Once again, Johnny did as he was asked. Reluctantly, Robert stepped into Grandpa's clasped hands and clung tightly to Grandpa's shoulders. "Now turn and put your hands on the tree," Grandpa said. Still reluctant, with one hand at a time, Robert let go of Grandpa and gripped the tree for dear life.

In the meantime, James climbed nearly to the top of the tree and began tossing large lemons to the ground. He looked down at his little brother from his lofty perch and said, "Come on Robert, don't be such a sissy."

"That's enough out of you, James," Grandpa grunted. Then, to Robert, he said, "Come on Robert; step up there with Johnny, before you break my back." Robert tentatively stepped onto the bough next to Johnny, wrapped both arms around a large limb and stood there frozen. He held on so tightly that his knuckles turned white. Grandpa let out a sigh and said, "Come on, I'll help you back down."

"See, I told you he was a sissy," James said triumphantly.

Grandpa looked up at James and asked, "When is the last time that you've had a good whipping?"

Robert reached out, plucked a lemon from the nearest branch and lobbed it up at his brother, striking him square in the center of his back. James instinctively reached for a lemon in retaliation. Grandpa quickly interjected, "I wouldn't if I were you, young man! As I see it, you had that coming." James frowned and let the lemon slip from his fingers to the ground. Feeling more confident, Robert continued to pick lemons next to Johnny. Grandpa sat down at the base of the tree and leaned his back against the trunk. Lemons rained down from the tree all around him.

Mrs. Bailey emerged from the house with a large bucket, a quarter of the way filled with ice. She chuckled at the sight of them as she walked up to the tree. Grandpa struggled up from the ground and said, "That will do, you guys." Grandpa helped Robert down first, and then Johnny. James climbed down to the lowest bough and then jumped to the ground. Grandpa looked around the base of the tree and sheepishly said to Mrs. Bailey, "I hope you needed some lemons too?"

Again, she chuckled and said, "I can certainly use a couple, but you guys go ahead and take the rest. And when you're ready for it, you can come back over and get some more ice."

Grandpa stooped down, gathered up a hand full of lemons for her and handed them to her.

She took them and said, "Thank you," and then walked back to the house.

"How are we going to carry all of these back?" asked Robert.

Grandpa walked over to Robert and said, "You take your left hand and hold the bottom of your shirt." Robert did as he was instructed. "That's it," Grandpa said, encouraging him. "Now lift it up to the middle of your belly and you can load it up with lots of lemons." The boys picked up the rest of the lemons off the ground and used the front of their shirts, just like Grandpa had told them. Then, all four of them walked back to the camp. When they arrived back, the three boys gathered around Grandpa, and with great anticipation, watched him slice the lemons. At the first whiff of the acidic fruit, their saliva glands kicked in. Johnny licked his lips and stepped closer. Grandpa looked up at him and smiled.

"James, could you go fetch the sugar from my place?" James turned and sprinted to Grandpa's shack. He bound up the steps like a deer and was back in a flash with the bag of sugar; as if he was afraid that he would miss something.

Grandpa piled the sliced lemons on top of the ice and quite liberally poured the sugar over the lemons. He walked over for a pail of water from the water barrel. The three boys took this opportunity to walk up and peer into the bucket. Their eyes brightened at the site of the sugar, wet and glistening on top of the lemons. The strong pungent aroma of the lemons made their mouths go wild with sensation. They stepped back to make room for Grandpa, when he walked back over to them with the water. He poured water over his concoction carefully. Then, he picked up his ladle and stirred it slowly at first, and then more vigorously. The boys stood transfixed, watching him. Grandpa looked up at them and asked, "Where are your cups?"

The boys scattered and ran for the shacks. James was the first one back. Panting like one of the dogs on a hot day, he held his cup out to Grandpa. Grandpa filled it all the way to the top. James grinned and said, "Thank you Grandpa, you're the best."

"You're welcome, son."

James gulped down the sweet, tart treat and was on his second fill up by the time the other two boys returned. Johnny and Robert both held their cups out over the bucket and Grandpa filled them with his ladle until they were overflowing. The two little ones smiled and eagerly drank it down. Grandpa watched and smiled at the sight of lemonade flowing out the corners of their mouths and dripping off their chins. Grandpa looked down the long dirt road and saw a plume of dust growing thicker as it came toward them. "It looks like your folks are back," he told the boys. They turned and followed his gaze with their own. "Do you think they will be thirsty?"

The boys unanimously nodded in agreement. Johnny piped up and said, "I know Mommy likes lemonade."

Robert gleefully added, "Look, we still have almost a whole bucket full."

The car pulled up closer, slowing until it rolled to a stop. The two young ones set their cups down on the table and made a beeline for the car. The doors swung open and the adults stepped out with their arms full of groceries.

Robert ran up to Buster and boasted, "Daddy, I climbed Mrs. Bailey's lemon tree."

Buster looked down at his son's happy face and he reached out and affectionately roughed up Robert's hair saying, "Wow, you did?"

"I sure did," Robert said proudly.

Johnny took Lilly by the hand and led her over to the bucket sitting on the table. He told her on the way over from the car, "We climbed the tree and picked some lemons, Mommy, so that we could make you some lemonade."

When they reached the table, Lilly kneeled down, wrapped her arms around him and whispered into his ear, "I love you," and then she kissed him on his ear lobe.

"Were they any trouble, Grandpa, while we were gone?" Beth asked.

"Oh heck, Beth, they pretty much took care of me."

"I wish it was that easy when I look after them," Beth said, looking at her boys and smiling. They both walked over and leaned up against their mother. She put an arm around each of their shoulders and pulled them in closer to her. The three of them stood like that for a long while.

"I know you all must be thirsty after that drive," Grandpa said, giving the lemonade a good stir.

"You bet," Buster said, running his tongue over his parched lips.

"I'll get all your cups," James volunteered.

"Thank you, James," Lilly said, sitting down upon one of the benches at the table. James returned with their cups and everyone had some of the sweet tart liquid.

The next morning Buster got out of bed ahead of everyone else and started the fire for their breakfast. Grandpa woke up and moaned as he climbed out of his bed. He was very stiff this morning and his body seemed to ache just about everywhere. He was the next one to emerge from his shack. "Good morning," he said to Buster, as he approached the fire.

"Good morning, Grandpa. The coffee is almost ready. Would you like a cup?"

"That sounds mighty fine to me," Grandpa replied, and groaned when he sat down in his chair. Buster looked at him with concern. "Just old age caching up with me, I'm afraid."

"Did you sleep wrong?"

"I reckon I did. I just feel like I've been whipped all over."

"I didn't get much sleep myself."

Grandpa looked up at him. "Go on," Grandpa said, encouraging him.

"Beth wept most of the night, it seemed. This whole thing is just about killing her."

"Beth and Lilly have grown to be like sisters. Heck, it's all I can do to take it myself," Grandpa stated.

"I hear you," Buster said.

Buster's two boys were the next up. They walked up to the fire, rubbing the sleep from their eyes. "Daddy, we tried to wake Mommy up, but she wouldn't budge," James said.

"Well, let her sleep in for a bit. She didn't sleep well last night."

"Who's going to help Grandpa with breakfast?" Robert asked.

Buster smiled at his two boys and said, "Believe it or not, I used to have to cook to feed myself before I met your mother."

Grandpa chuckled and said, "And he's still here to tell about it; amazing isn't it?"

"It sure is," James said.

"You two boys go over to the hen house and fetch us some eggs, and I will show you just what I can do," Buster said. "Do you have any more of that salt pork left?" Buster asked Grandpa.

"I do. How much do you need?"

"I figure just a couple of thin slices. I'm going to boil some of the salt out, and dice it up to go into some scrambled eggs."

Grandpa groaned again as he got up from his chair. "I'll fix some of my grits to go with them eggs of yours, so we don't need to bother the women folk this morning."

"It sounds like a good plan, Grandpa, thank you."

Grandpa simply nodded and hobbled off to his shack. The two boys watched as Grandpa made his way, more slowly than usual. Robert was the one to ask the question, "What's wrong with Grandpa?"

"It's old age," his father answered.

"But he's been old for a long time," James said.

"That is true, but this morning he's feeling older than usual, that's all. Now, if you two would like some breakfast, you best get to gathering the eggs."

James walked over to the end of the table and picked up the egg basket. Robert sprinted off toward the chicken coop and shouted back over his shoulder. "I'll race you and the last one is a rotten egg."

James didn't take the bait. He just sighed and walked at his own pace. When James reached the chicken coop, Robert already had the old broom in his hands. "I'll stand guard while you gather the eggs," he told his brother.

James looked at Robert warily and said, "You know what happened the last time I trusted you to stand guard. The first time that old rooster flew at you, you dropped the broom and ran screaming like a girl, and he darned near got me."

Chapter 6

"I know, but you can trust me this time."

"How is this time going to be any different than last time?"

"This time, I will be ready for that old cock. I'll bat him out of the air just like he is a baseball."

"Okay, but this is your last chance. If that rooster gets me, you're gathering the eggs from here on out. Is that a deal?"

"You've got yourself a deal."

"Fair enough, be on your guard," James said, before opening the door "After you," James continued. Robert hesitated, and then took a deep breath and stepped through the doorway, waving the broom wildly as he did so. James stepped in behind his little brother and closed the door behind them.

The rooster ruffled his feathers to make himself appear larger and looked down at them with his head cocked sideways from his perch in the rafters. He eyed them with great suspicion. "Don't take your eyes off him; not even for one second," James cautioned.

"I got you covered," Robert answered nervously, doubting himself.

James began to collect the eggs, making for some very angry hens. The rooster began to strut back and forth and once spread his wings to make a descent, but Robert didn't hesitate. He swung the broom at the rooster and the rooster flapped his wings, making himself airborne only long enough to avoid a blow. "I nearly got him," Robert said gleefully.

"I don't care, just as long as he doesn't fly at me," James said, shooting the rooster a nervous glance.

Robert smiled. He was very proud of himself for standing his ground the way he did. "Momma says that he would taste mighty good in a pot with some dumplings."

James shot the rooster another look and simply said, "He's too tough, a younger one would be better."

"But where is the satisfaction of eating a younger one? This one has some cantankerous history."

"I'll give you that," James said, agreeing with his younger sibling.

The rooster opened his beak and snapped at the air between Robert and the broom, threateningly. "Are you almost done collecting those eggs? I don't know how much longer I can hold him off."

"I'm almost done," James said.

Just then, the rooster flew from his perch and landed on top of the bristles of the broom. Robert screamed and threw rooster, broom and all up against the wall. The rooster slid limply down the wall and James nearly dropped the eggs. He looked at the rooster and said, "I think he is dead."

Robert nodded in agreement and said, "Dumplings tonight."

Buster looked up at the two boys approaching the fire and said, "What the heck?"

Grandpa followed his gaze and smiled. James walked toward them with the egg basket and Robert followed holding the old rooster upside down by its scrawny legs. "I've wanted to do that myself for a long time," Grandpa said.

"What on earth happened?" Buster exclaimed. "I asked you boys to gather some eggs; not the eggs and their daddy too."

"It was that old rooster's own doing," James said, defending his little brother.

"Yeah, I was just protecting James, and that old rooster went and got himself killed."

"Yeah, that's all there was to it!" James said.

"That's all there was to it, huh?" Buster asked skeptically.

"Yes sir," Robert said, and James shook his head in agreement.

Robert walked up and handed his father the limp rooster. "Momma always said she wanted to make some dumplings out of him."

Buster couldn't help but to smile and took the rooster from Robert. "Grandpa, would you mind walking this bird over to Mrs. Bailey's, to put him into her icebox?"

Grandpa said, "She won't mind, she likes chicken and dumplings. You boys want to come along? She would love to hear your story."

"Sure, I can tell her how I fought him off and saved James," Robert said, as the two boys fell in alongside Grandpa while they walked toward Mrs. Bailey's house. Buster chuckled as he watched them go, and then he went back to tending to breakfast.

Beth walked up to the table and asked, "Where are those three off to?"

Buster looked down the road at the three, now distant figures. "Robert clubbed himself a rooster this morning."

"Robert?"

"Yes, Robert."

"Is it dead?"

"Yes it is."

"It's had it coming for a long time," Beth said.

"Robert said you wanted to make some chicken and dumplings out of him."

"I do."

"Well now you have your chance. They're taking it to Mrs. Bailey's icebox until you're ready for it." Buster put his arms around her and pulled her to him. "How are you doing this morning, baby?" he asked, and brushed his lips across her forehead.

She rested her head against his big barrel chest and said, "I'll be okay, I reckon."

"I hear you, baby." He gave her a squeeze and turned her loose.

"Thank you for cooking this morning."

"Don't mention it. I'm glad to help out."

They both saw Johnny and Lilly descending the steps of their shack. Buster swallowed, but his throat still felt dry. Beth stepped closer to him and nervously took his hand. He gave it a gentle squeeze, reassuring her. Beth let go of his hand and, as if he had given her strength, she found the courage to walk forward and greet Johnny and Lilly. She put an arm around a shoulder of each one and embraced them. They returned her embrace and the three of them stood like that for a long while. Beth first kissed Lilly's cheek, and then released her to stoop and kiss Johnny's tear streaked cheeks. She gave him one more hug and together they walked up to the fire.

Buster handed each woman a cup of hot coffee and said, "Good morning."

Johnny just nodded sullenly, acknowledging Buster.

"Good morning, Buster. Thank you for the coffee," Lilly said.

"He made us some breakfast too," Beth said.

"Coffee will be good for me, this morning," Lilly said, "but thank you, just the same."

"But you need something to keep up your strength," Beth protested.

"I'll be fine, really."

"Lilly, Beth is right," Buster coaxed her.

"But my stomach is all in knots, I don't think I can keep anything down."

The dogs ran up to the table and surrounded Johnny, wagging their tails and licking at his hands. He smiled down at them and wondered how did they know? How did they know that he was leaving soon? He squatted down and let them shower him with kisses. Soon, his tear-streaked cheeks were bright and shiny. Johnny stood up and saw Grandpa and his two friends walking up the road toward them. He ran to meet them, with the dogs bounding all around him. Johnny heard all about the rooster incident and wished that he had gotten up early enough to see it for himself. He marveled at the thought of Robert protecting James. It must have really been something to see. Even James seemed proud of Robert.

Buster served everyone up. Grandpa fussed about being waited on, but Buster wouldn't hear it. He put a plate in front of Lilly and simply said, "Just do the best you can."

She looked up at him, nodded and said, "Thank you." She nibbled at the food, but mostly just did a lot of moving it around on her plate.

Once everyone was done with breakfast, Johnny looked in the direction of King's cage and said to his two friends, "Do you reckon that we should go find King some breakfast?"

James said, "Sure, it's been awhile since he's had anything to eat."

The three of them headed in the direction of the goat pen and started to scout around for breakfast prospects for the lizard. After a bit of rummaging around, turning over old pieces of wood and other odds and ends that lay about, Robert called out, "Look here at what I found. King is sure going to eat well today."

James looked down at a long line of red ants. They were big and fearsome looking. "Those will bite us. I'm not touching them."

"They are harvester ants," Robert said.

63

"I don't care what kind of ants they are; I'm not going to touch them. You go right ahead if you want too, mister smarty pants."

While the two brothers verbally sparred back and forth, Johnny looked for a solution to their situation and he found it. Johnny picked up an old tin can and a small thin piece of wood. "Look, I found the answer." The two boys stopped their bickering and turned toward Johnny. "Watch," Johnny said, while he bent down and ran the lip of the old can along the long trail of ants, scooping them up, sand and all. He then quickly capped it with the piece of wood and stood up and grinned at his friends. "Mission accomplished."

"That was easy. Why didn't I think of that?" Robert said, shaking his head in wonder. James simply smirked at him and then let it go.

They walked over to King's cage and Johnny said, "If one of you will open the door, I can give these to him."

"How are you going to do that without getting bit?" James asked.

"Just open the door and I will show you." James did as he was asked and opened the door. Johnny slipped the can inside the cage and sat it down, removing the lid and dropping it next to the can when he saw ants on the bottom of it.

The boys sat down in a semicircle around the cage cross-legged like three little Indians and waited patiently. They sat very still and quiet. Soon, ants were emerging from the can and crawling down its sides.

Shortly thereafter, King caught sight of movement outside his little makeshift cave and poked his head out into the sunlight. He flickered his reptilian tongue once, honing in on his unsuspecting prey, and then, with surprising speed and deadly accuracy, he flicked his tongue again and swallowed an ant whole. Then, before you could blink an eye, a second ant had disappeared off the side of the can. The boys began to squirm with excitement when they saw two more disappear down King's throat.

Finally, Johnny could no longer contain himself, "He loves them!" he exclaimed.

"He sure does," Robert agreed.

"Well, it sure is going to be easy to feed him from now on. We have those darn ants all over this place," James said.

Then, in a sullen tone Robert asked, "Johnny, is it true that you and Lilly are going to leave here?"

Johnny's mood changed instantly. He grew sad and looked from his hungry reptile into the eyes of his youngest friend. The sadness in Robert's eyes mirrored his own. "I sure don't want to go anywhere, especially if it is anywhere without you guys."

James said, "I know, maybe we can talk Lilly out of it. I don't think she really wants to leave either."

"I know she doesn't, but Grandpa says that it is the best thing for us."

"Hog wash, the best thing for you to do is to stay here with your friends," James said, taking command of the conversation.

"He says that it is best for our future."

"That's stuff that only makes sense to grownups," Robert said. "What good is a future if you can't have your friends in it?"

"Even if we have to leave, which I don't want to, you two will always be my friends; I swear." All three boys then fell into each other's arms in a group hug.

Buster said to Beth, "I'll go over to Mrs. Bailey's and clean up that rooster for you, Beth."

"Thank you, Buster. He was a tough old thing; he'll need to stew for quite awhile. Would you please invite Mrs. Bailey to join us for dinner?"

Buster kissed her lightly on the mouth and said, "I will." He turned and headed up the road, toward the boss lady's house. When Buster got back from taking care of the rooster over at Mrs. Bailey's house, Buster said to his wife, "Mrs. Bailey said that she would love to come for supper this evening. She said that you make the best chicken and dumplings that she has ever tasted in her long life."

Beth smiled and said, "Oh, she is just being kind."

Buster stepped behind Beth, wrapped his arms around her slim waist and nestled his face into her hair and whispered, "She is a truthful woman. You are the best in both our books."

Beth stepped out of his embrace and swatted him playfully with her dishtowel. "Make use of yourself and go do your choirs."

Buster was walking past the boys at King's cage when Robert asked, "Daddy, can't you talk some sense into Grandpa?"

"What are you talking about?"

"That notion of his, that Johnny and Lilly will be happier without us."

"He didn't say that they will be happier."

"Well then, that settles it," Robert said triumphantly. "They should stay!"

Buster roughed up his youngest son's hair and said, "It's not that simple, sport."

James chimed in and said, "Why do adults always have to make everything complicated?"

"Life is just more complex than it appears on the surface," his father said.

James furrowed his eyebrows and replied, "I just don't get it."

"You will when you get older." Buster said and went about his chores.

With the chicken and dumplings done at last, they all sat around the table waiting for Grandpa and Mrs. Bailey. Grandpa pulled up in Mrs. Bailey's car, with Mrs. Bailey sitting by his side. He opened her door for her and escorted her to the table. Buster got up from the table and heaped large portions into everyone's bowls. He sat a bowl down in front of Mrs. Bailey first. She said, "Oh, Buster, I can never finish all that. I don't want to be wasteful."

Buster smiled at her and said, "It has been a long while since you have had Beth's chicken and dumplings." He placed bowls in front of everyone else and then sat down to join them. Everyone ate with relish; even Lilly, who had hardly touched any food the day before. Buster looked over at Mrs. Bailey's empty bowl and smiled. "Would you like more, Mrs. Bailey?"

"Oh, you were so right, Buster. Beth, I just plumb forgot what an amazing cook you truly are."

"Why, thank you, Mrs. Bailey. You are too kind."

"Oh, nonsense, it is the plain truth. Buster here is a lucky man."

"Would you like more?" Buster asked her again.

"I would love more, but I couldn't possibly eat anymore. I already feel like I'm going to bust a seam."

Simultaneously Buster's two boys picked up their bowls and held them out to their father. "We'll have more, Daddy," James said. Buster refilled their bowls, and then his own and Grandpa's.

At last, Grandpa said. "Beth, if I had known that old rooster would taste so darn good, I would have clubbed him myself for you long ago."

Beth looked across the table at Grandpa and smiled. "I bet that I could make some amazing meals out of that old billy goat, Rex."

Robert piped up and said, "Nobody would miss him, Grandpa."

Grandpa looked at Robert in mock surprise and said, "You're taking the side of a woman? We men are supposed to stick together."

Robert said, "She's my momma and she would cook him up right." Everyone around the table laughed.

Johnny said, "No one would miss that old billy goat. He is nothing but trouble."

Grandpa came to the defense of Rex and said, "All of his girlfriends would miss him."

James said, "Grandpa, I think you are the only one that would miss him." Almost everyone around the table shook their heads in agreement with James' statement.

Later that evening at the dinner table, James tried to bring up the subject of Johnny and Lilly leaving again. "Why do you want to leave, Lilly?"

"James," Beth said sternly, "not tonight, we have company."

Mrs. Bailey said, "It's alright, Beth. The child has the right to ask questions."

"She's right," Grandpa added.

"This is a hard decision for all of us to make," Lilly said.

"Just don't make it and everything will be fine," Robert pleaded.

Lilly looked down at her plate and said, "I just wish it were that simple."

"See, there the adults go, just complicating things up again! It is just that simple!" James stated.

"Young man, you had just better hold your tongue!" Buster warned James.

Lilly came to James's defense and said, "Buster, he didn't mean any disrespect by it. He has a right to his feelings."

Johnny broke his silence and said, "Mommy, I'm going to lose all my friends."

Lilly looked across the table at her son and tears slipped from the corners of her eyes as she said, "Me too, Johnny, but they will always be in our hearts."

Beth sniffled back her own tears and said, "I can't take any more of this tonight. Let's just all eat our supper."

"Amen," Buster said. The rest of them all chimed in together and said, "Amen," so the subject was dropped for the rest of the evening.

When everyone was done eating, Beth and Lilly got up to clear the table and Mrs. Bailey got up to help them. Beth took the bowls from her hands and said, "Mrs. Bailey, you are our guest. I won't have you cleaning up."

Grandpa said, "Mrs. Bailey, come over here and join me and Buster at the fire."

"But I should be helping Beth clean up, not Lilly."

Lilly walked over and gave Mrs. Bailey a hug. "You have already done so much for me, and I shall always be so grateful. You just go over there and relax and enjoy your evening. I need something to do anyhow."

"Okay, my dear, only if you insist."

"I do."

Mrs. Bailey nodded and turned towards the fire. Grandpa seated her in his own chair. After Lilly and Beth finished their evening chores, they joined the others at the fire.

"Lilly, my dear, you will write often and keep us posted on how you and Johnny are getting along?" Mrs. Bailey asked.

Lilly replied, "Of course I will. All of you here are really all the family that Johnny and I have."

A little while later Mrs. Bailey said. "I'm plumb tuckered out."

Grandpa got up from his chair and extended a hand to Mrs. Bailey. "Well then, I shall take the lady home."

Mrs. Bailey stood and then turned to Lilly. "Lilly, you have a safe journey and remember, as soon as you get to Fort Bragg, write to us."

Lilly stood and gave Mrs. Bailey a big hug. "I promise, I will."

Mrs. Bailey then turned to Beth and said, "Beth, the meal this evening was lovely, thank you."

"The pleasure is mine, Mrs. Bailey. Thank you for joining us," Beth replied.

"Have a good night, everyone," Mrs. Bailey said, as she walked arm-in-arm with Grandpa to her car.

"Good night, Mrs. Bailey," everyone called from around the fire.

The next morning the three boys were trying to feed King his breakfast. They had caught him a beetle on this morning. King was sunning himself on the large flat stone that served as the roof of his cave. He watched the beetle with disinterest, as it crawled about his cage looking for an escape route. It soon found one and crawled through the wire of the cage. Robert scurried to catch it.

"Oh, let it go," James said.

Robert looked at his brother, not quite believing what he just heard. "Why?" he asked.

"Clearly, King is not hungry."

"How do you know?" Robert demanded.

Johnny answered for James, "The last time we caught him the same type of beetle, he ate it right away. Did you see how many ants he ate yesterday?"

"Yeah, he was a pig, alright," Robert said.

Johnny replied, "His belly probably hurts. We'll try feeding him again tonight. I can tell you guys will take good care of King."

Robert perked up and his eyes were bright and shiny when he asked Johnny, "You're going to give him to us?"

Chapter 7

"I sure am. He is the King of the desert. He wouldn't be happy anywhere else. Just because I have to leave my friends, it doesn't mean that he has to leave his desert."

"Wow!" Robert exclaimed, and went running to the fire, calling out in his excitement, "Daddy, Mommy, guess what?"

Johnny watched his youngest friend sprint off and he felt mixed emotions. He was happy that he could do this for his friends, but it meant now he would be leaving just one more thing that he loved behind. Life was becoming very complicated. He guessed that he was just growing up too fast this past week.

"Thank you," James said.

"Huh?" Johnny had been lost deep in his thoughts, with his emotions swirling around him like a silent dust devil.

"Robert forgot to say thank you, because he was so excited. I was just saying thank you for both of us. We will take the best care of him."

"I know that you will."

"Grandpa said that it is much cooler there where you are going. It is good for King that you are leaving him here," James said, trying to make his friend feel better about his decision. Johnny just nodded.

After a bit, Robert ran back toward them. "Breakfast is ready, you guys."

The boys walked over to the table and Robert spied biscuits piled high on a plate sitting on the table. "Is there gravy too?"

"There sure is," Grandpa said proudly. "Mrs. Bailey let me use her oven this morning, so I pulled out all the stops."

"Yeah, it was easy for Grandpa," Buster said.

Robert turned and looked at his father and smiled saying, "He made you milk the nanny?"

Buster nodded and said, "I only did it for Lilly," and then Buster winked at Lilly. Lilly smiled across the table at him.

"Are you trying to get her into trouble?" Grandpa said to Buster. "You know what a vicious wildcat your woman can be."

Beth said, "The only one that is going to get into trouble is him."

Grandpa said, "I think he needs to milk that nanny more often. It will tame her down a wee bit."

Buster pulled up his pants leg and revealed an angry looking bruise on his lower calf. "Look here, Beth honey, I risked life and limb just to bring a little goat milk to your table."

"Don't you honey me! I'm in agreement with Grandpa, I could get used to having some milk for my coffee."

Just to stir things up a little more, Grandpa added, "Besides, Buster, if you get that nanny tamed down enough, James could take to milking her when you're gone to the cotton gin."

James shot Grandpa a dark look and said, "You're always thinking, Grandpa."

Grandpa smiled at him and said, "You like gravy?"

"Well maybe, if you make me biscuits to go with it."

"I can work that out with Mrs. Bailey," Grandpa replied.

"It's looking bad for you, Dad," Robert said.

"What are you talking about, Robert? Are you saying that you are siding with them?"

Robert shook his head and said, "For biscuits and gravy, heck yeah, you bet I am."

"You sure sell out pretty darn cheaply," Buster said. Robert just grinned at his father.

Beth brought a large bowl of gravy with salt pork in it to the table and set it down in front of the boys. Johnny's mouth watered and he said, "Beth that sure does look good." She smiled at him and handed him a ladle. As Johnny scooped the gravy onto his plate, Lilly passed the biscuits to Beth's boys.

After they were done with breakfast, Beth said, "Grandpa, you sure did look sweet on Mrs. Bailey last night."

"Now look at the way you act, after I go through great trouble to get you milk for your coffee. After all she is a widow."

"The way I heard it, Daddy went through the trouble," Robert said.

"Are you two ganging up on me?"

"If my mama needs back up, you bet," Robert said to Grandpa, with a wide grin.

"Son, your mamma has never needed any back up," Grandpa replied.

Beth brought Grandpa's fire stick over to him and handed it to him. "You see how pushy she can be too?"

"James could you and Robert fetch me some more water from the well, please?"

"Oh, Momma," Robert whined.

Grandpa chuckled and said, "See."

"We are running low on water. Now get!" Beth said firmly.

Reluctantly, Beth's two boys got up and each took a water bucket and headed toward the well. Johnny picked up a third bucket and followed behind.

73

Grandpa got up, walked over to the fire and gave it a good stir, and then piled on some twigs, which caused smoke to billow up into his face. He coughed and walked over to the wood pile for some larger pieces.

The next morning was an emotional one for everyone, as they helped Johnny and Lilly prepare for their long trip. Beth cooked up a lot of extra fry bread, wrapped it up with all the dry meat that they had and handed to Lilly. "This will get you both most of the way there," Beth said.

Lilly broke into tears, "I hate this, Beth, us leaving all of you here."

"Me too, Lilly, I hate it too!" Beth said, and took Lilly into her arms. The two friends stood there and cried on each other's shoulder.

Johnny and his two friends sat huddled around King's cage. Finally, Robert asked Johnny, "Can't you talk your mamma out of leaving?"

Sadly, Johnny shook his head and said, "No, because I know she doesn't want to go, but I just don't understand grown-ups."

"I don't understand them either," James said. "If she doesn't want to go, she should just stay!"

"I've already tried my very best to tell her that!" Johnny said.

"What did she say?" Robert asked.

"She said that she wished it was that simple," Johnny said.

"See, what I told you! Grown-ups are just so dang confusing!" James said.

"Do you guys suppose there are any lizards in Fort Bragg?" Johnny asked his friends, while looking sadly at King.

There was a long pause of silence and then James jumped up and said, "I don't know the answer to that, but I know who would."

Johnny looked up at his friend and smiled, "Grandpa?"

Robert jumped to his feet and answered the question with one word, "Yup."

This time Johnny jumped to his feet and the three friends went racing toward the fire pit, where Grandpa was doing the morning clean up from breakfast, with the help of Buster. "Grandpa, Grandpa!" all three boys were shouting excitedly.

Grandpa looked toward the rapidly approaching youngsters. He then looked at Buster and said, "What the Sam Hill is going on?"

Buster merely shrugged his shoulders and said, "I don't have a clue."

James was the first one to reach Grandpa. "Does Fort Bragg have lizards? You said King would die if Johnny took him there."

"Well sure it has lizards. The climate is just too cold for the type of lizard that King is."

"What kind of lizards does it have, Grandpa?" Johnny asked excitedly.

"Well it has blue belly lizards, and another lizard-like creature which is very interesting, called a salamander, that has smooth skin and likes water and mud."

Robert said, "It will be great Johnny, if you can find either one of those."

Johnny's little face lit up and he said, "That would sure be swell." His two friends nodded in wholehearted agreement.

Grandpa turned toward Beth and Lilly and said, "Lilly, as much as it breaks my heart to say so, the two of you had best get going. That is a long trip."

Beth reluctantly agreed with Grandpa and said, "Lilly, he is right."

Lilly smiled weakly at her two dear friends and said, "I guess I have put it off just as long as I possibly could."

"We have, too," Beth said.

"Johnny we have to get going."

Johnny and Lilly hugged all their friends and said tearful goodbyes, and then climbed into the old Ford. The small group huddled together and watched them go. The Ford steadfastly made its way down the highway and Johnny was the first to break the silence. "Momma, do you think I will make new friends in Fort Bragg."

Lilly quickly glanced at him and said, "Of course you will. And so will I, but we will always have our dear friends here in the desert." The miles slid behind them as the Ford held its course, with its nose pointed west. After a few hours on the road, Lilly could see brightly colored fields on either side of the highway. She leaned back deeper into her seat and smiled. She loved flowers. As they drew closer, she first checked her side mirror and then the rear one, and then she slowed the car down so she could get a better look.

"What's wrong?" Johnny asked.

"Nothing is wrong, Johnny, I just wanted to get a good look at those flowers. Do you remember the story that Grandpa told all you children, about the old Indian Chief that was buried with his magic blanket?"

Johnny's face brightened and he said, "I sure do."

"Those are the flowers in his story. Those are the Indian blankets."

Johnny peered out the windows of the car at the massive fields of flowers and said, "Wow, then that was a true story."

Lilly couldn't help but to chuckle a bit and then she said, "Apparently, it was a true story, because there they are." She picked back up her speed and all too soon the beautiful flower fields vanished into the distance behind them. Johnny leaned back in his seat and smiled as he daydreamed about his upcoming seaside adventure.

Please write a review on Amazon or Goodreads. It will be greatly appreciated.

There are six books in 'Johnny's Adventure' series; #1 'Johnny's Reptile Adventure', #2 'The Skipper's Captain', #3 'The Heroic Dog and Boy', #4 'Finding A Home', #5 'The Magic Wishbone', and #6 'Johnny's Treasure Adventure'.

Made in the USA
Las Vegas, NV
30 December 2021

39846276R00049